The Raging Vortex

S. VATSAL

BLUEROSE PUBLISHERS
India | U.K.

Copyright © S. Vatsal 2025

All rights reserved by author. No part of this publication may be reproduced, stored in a retrieval system or transmitted in any form or by any means, electronic, mechanical, photocopying, recording or otherwise, without the prior permission of the author. Although every precaution has been taken to verify the accuracy of the information contained herein, the publisher assumes no responsibility for any errors or omissions. No liability is assumed for damages that may result from the use of information contained within.

BlueRose Publishers takes no responsibility for any damages, losses, or liabilities that may arise from the use or misuse of the information, products, or services provided in this publication.

For permissions requests or inquiries regarding this publication, please contact:

BLUEROSE PUBLISHERS
www.BlueRoseONE.com
info@bluerosepublishers.com
+91 8882 898 898
+4407342408967

ISBN: 978-93-6783-677-4

Cover design: Yash Singhal
Typesetting: Namrata Saini

First Edition: January 2025

Dedicated with love and fond remembrances to pure angels, who once walked this earth...

Lily J. Devi, my loving grandma,

And,

Dr. Laxminarayan, my scholarly grandpa.

You continue to inspire.

Much gratitude and special thanks to my noble Dad, my loving doctor Mom, my children...Anayna and Ashish, my spouse, my kind scholarly uncle Shree Harsh, my beautiful aunt Renuji and all family members who have been my rock support in this incredible journey of penning down the novel.

My gratitude also to readers and lovers of fiction books.

Special mention and thanks to Ashish Aryan and Anayna Nidhi Singh for the editing work.

CONTENTS

Chapter One: The Hidden Quest — 1

Chapter Two: The Prying Eye — 9

Chapter Three: Brief Encounter Amidst Madness — 13

Chapter Four: The Innocent Acquaintance — 18

Chapter Five: Conspiracy of the Astral-Venus Plexus — 23

Chapter Six: The Retro Journey With Hazel — 27

Chapter Seven: Challenges from the Mafia — 34

Chapter Eight: The Pique Selection — 38

Chapter Nine: Mission Unfolds — 40

Chapter Ten: Clandestine Escapade — 46

Chapter Eleven: The Final Goodbye — 50

Chapter Twelve: Rachel's Ascent — 53

Chapter Thirteen: The Nine Unknown Men And Marc — 56

Chapter Fourteen: The Meeting of Genius Minds — 61

Chapter Fifteen: Big Betrayal From The Brutal Heart — 64

Chapter Sixteen: The Game Begins — 70

Chapter Seventeen: Reading God's Mind — 79

Chapter Eighteen: The Pursuit of The Elusive — 89

Chapter Nineteen: The Night of Tempest — 96

Chapter Twenty: Puppets of Machiavellian Chamaeleon — 107

Chapter Twenty-One: Unveiling Secrets in Holiday Home — 113

Chapter Twenty-Two: The Crystal Ball Gazing — 120

Chapter Twenty-Three: The Twist in the Double Game — 129

Chapter Twenty-Four: The Premonition — 133

Chapter Twenty-Five: The Vanishing Silhouettes —— 138

Chapter Twenty-Six: Slow Dance with the Enemy —— 141

Chapter Twenty-Seven: Anahata, The Unhurt, The Unbeaten —— 144

Chapter Twenty-Eight: Forging New Alliance —— 150

Chapter Twenty-Nine: Falling in Love with The Enemy —— 154

Chapter Thirty: The Juggernaut Feat —— 163

Chapter Thirty-One: Clinging on to Last Straw of Hope —— 166

Chapter Thirty-Two: The Phoenix Arisen —— 172

Chapter Thirty-Three: The Perfect Imperfect Fragile Life —— 176

CHAPTER ONE
THE HIDDEN QUEST

In the hustle and bustle of the city that never sleeps... New York, a man moved with purpose through the crowded halls of Penn Station. His name was Victor, a dashing intelligence officer with the charisma of a Broadway star. As the clock struck ten on the cold pre-Halloween night of October, his mission was far from over, and he had little time to waste.

The station's vibrant lights flickered above him, casting fleeting shadows on his defined features and impeccably done-up hair. The Burberry Classic Trench coat that gracefully draped his tall, lean figure billowed slightly as he walked swiftly. There was an air of mystery about this man, a certain kind of enigma beneath his charming façade.

Like a ghost, he seamlessly weaved through the sea of people. He seemed engrossed in an important conversation over the cell phone which he held close to his ear, but he was hardly audible to the people around. A woman's crisp voice over the phone resonated in his ears and he listened intently. She spoke of things that gnawed at her heart, but it apparently had little impact on Victor. There was nothing new in what she conveyed. Victor already knew everything about it. However, he patiently listened to her as she spoke. Once she had paused, Victor spoke to her in hushed voice with conviction,

"Clara dear, please don't talk to anyone else about it. It's only between you and me, ok. You must understand that privacy is power in our profession. People cannot destroy what they do not know. I hope I'm clear... am I? Please...please...do take a restful sleep and stop worrying about my safety...ok! I'm on my guard at all times. Good night, sweet dreams!"

With that, Victor snapped the call. But, deep down in his heart, he knew Clara's forebodings were not unfounded, and he needed to be more cautious. Clara was a foreign operative whom Victor trusted. She was repeatedly warning him to be wary of beautiful strangers and silent pursuers. She foresaw them as instruments of disruption and destruction. She claimed they could be fatal for him.

"Actually, Clara had done the right thing by reminding me of the perils that lay ahead."

Victor pondered and mumbled to himself,

"Ah, how intuitive and caring Clara is! "She is absolutely irreplaceable".

"But of late, there have been obvious streaks of jealousy in her behavior. God forbid, not again...not her as well! I hope and pray she does not have any love interest in me. I don't want emotional attachments and complications in my profession... I can't afford to carry the load of emotional baggage."

Clara, a member of Victor's formidable network of agents, informants, and foreign operatives, had been by Victor's side through the past decade. In the world of espionage, such lasting associations and relationships was a rarity. Intelligence officials often severed ties with their agents and informers once a mission was accomplished; but it was not so in the case of Victor. There was something about Victor, which earned him the unwavering loyalty and trust of those around him, especially women.

Women were not only drawn to his mission but were attracted to the man himself; handsome as he was. Moreover, he was known too for his gentleness towards the fairer sex that was rooted in his deep respect for women in general. It was a trait, that set him apart in a profession where genuine regard for women was a rare commodity. Besides, being a lady's gentleman that he was, Victor also considered it a part of his job to go out of the way...often way too far to pamper and oblige these stressed-out lovely women in the intriguing game of espionage with occasional sweet nothings that blurred the thin line between duty and devotion. These sweet nothings worked like shots of dopamine and serotonin in the unpredictable lives of these women. No wonder, the women associated with him simply adored him and some secretly fell in love with him.

As Victor emerged from the station's iron grasp and the subway's snug embrace to finally surface on 34th Street, Midtown Manhattan, he met with the sight of the city's towering skyscrapers looming overhead.

Throngs of hurried pedestrians, wrapped in jackets against the autumn chill, rushed past him. Some women, however, couldn't help but paused to have a good look at him and even tried to win his attention in various sultry ways. But, Victor was least distracted by amorous advances of these gorgeous women who voyeuristically looked at him with interest through their slanting eye-lashes.

Victor was a man on a big mission. He had an important rendezvous with his hotel room on the 31st floor of the Renaissance Hotel. Time was of great essence, and he knew it. As he walked, his mind constantly calculated the odds, anticipating the moves of unseen adversaries, weighing the risks with every step.

Victor was now barely thirty feet away from his destination, the hotel. However, a sudden, subtle but undeniable feeling crept over him...a disturbing sense of being followed so, with a swift, calculated move he deviated from the path that directly led to the hotel.

Victor's sixth sense signaled a potential threat. A figure shrouded in the anonymity of a black suit had been trailing him ever since he had emerged from the subway. The shadow that mirrored Victor's every step whispered a tale of silent pursuit and was a matter of concern. Victor must evade the pursuer.

With a quick move, Victor veered into the sinuous alleys that crisscrossed the city. Once in the alleys, Victor sought the cover of darkness to assess the situation. The figure in the black suit, unyielding in its pursuit, maintained a discreet distance, moving in Victor's direction with eerie precision.

Faster and faster, Victor moved through the labyrinth, instinctively choosing the paths that twisted and turned; enough to disorient anyone attempting to follow. Victor glanced over his shoulder; the figure in black remained relentless, tailing Victor with a determined persistence, almost a silent shadow. It was obvious this was no ordinary pursuer.

With each twist and turn, Victor's mind raced, mapping out his strategy. Going by the past-experiences, Victor knew, the crowded streets and avenues were the places where he could seamlessly merge with the myriad faces. Therefore, with a final burst of speed, he darted into a crowded street and maneuvered in the sea of humanity towards a bustling avenue. A master of blending in, he used the human tide to obscure his trail, melting into the fabric of the city.

The figure in black, now more distant, grappled with the challenge of tailing Victor in the swarm of people. The teeming crowd, the ebb and flow of the metropolis and the city's ceaseless traffic became Victor's shield. The pursuer paused momentarily searching for the elusive Intelligence Officer, but Victor was nowhere in sight. Victor had successfully evaded the pursuit.

With a quick change of direction and a few hundred hurried steps, Victor slipped into the hotel premises, leaving behind the chaotic rhythm of Midtown Manhattan. As he stood in front of the Renaissance Hotel, the grand façade of the building, with its timeless charm, seemingly greeted him with assured promises of good times within its opulent folds. The doorman, ever-vigilant, held the door open with a respectful nod, unknowingly welcoming a man of immense importance.

In the elevator, Victor's reflection gazed back at him more pronounced than ever. He ran a hand through his hair, adjusting his tie with a sense of refinement. He then said aloud to himself,

"God, be kind to beautiful Clara and bless her. Please keep her safe."

The ascent to the 31st floor seemed to happen in a flash, and soon enough, he was standing before the door of his luxurious suite. It was a much-in-demand room with a splendid view of the panoramic Manhattan skyline.

Once inside his hotel room, Victor felt the weight of the world lift from his shoulders. However, this was no time for complacency. He sat at the work desk and opened his laptop, fingers darting on the keys with urgency.

He must decipher the fifth and the last puzzle in the series of five sets of mysterious puzzles posted on the internet. These puzzles, posted within a span of five weeks by unknown sources had taken the netizens by storm. The stated intent behind the posting of puzzles was to recruit 'intelligent individuals' by presenting a series of puzzles to solve and the enigmatic unknown sources maintained internet anonymity These mind-boggling puzzles were based on cryptography, the Fibonacci series, mathematics of quantum mechanics, and entailed knowledge of the ancient Vedas and Upanishads.

These puzzles called 'the most elaborate and mysterious puzzle of the internet age' were aptly listed as, one of the 'top five eeriest unsolved mysteries of the internet' by all major daily newspapers. As such, much speculation was rife as to its motive.

Many had speculated that the puzzles were a recruitment tool for the NSA, CIA, MIS, FBI or some mercenary group. Victor's mission was to find out the true-identity of the group responsible for posting the puzzles and their intent behind it; and this required Victor to somehow manage getting recruited by them. After succeeding in it, he must infiltrate the group to discover the plans and motives of the group.

Victor had solved four out of the five puzzles, but the solution to the last puzzle still eluded him. Victor knew it for sure that rest, too, would elude him until he found the solution. But at the same time, he also knew the fact too well; for someone in the world of espionage, the serendipity of getting a restful break, or even a brief respite, was only a quixotic wish...a preposterous presumption.

Even as the first rays of dawn painted the New York skyline with hues of gold, Victor sat deeply immersed in his work over the laptop. Now he was getting quite close to finding the solution to the fifth puzzle after continuously working for hours without a break... until the doorbell rang.

The person at the other side of the door announced, *"Room Service"*.

Victor glanced at his watch, a sophisticated spying device with connectivity to a miniature spy camera fitted over the number plate on the door of his room; it blended so perfectly that no one could tell it apart. He had carefully mounted it there the day he had checked in.

The watch screen displayed the person waiting outside the room; she was the same hotel employee, the room attendant who had been at service since he checked in. The room attendant was standing demurely in the doorway. Victor opened the door and let her in. Polite, pretty and petite, she greeted him in the sweetest voice,

"Good morning."

She trotted across the room and placed the tray with teapots, cups and goodies on the side table by the window. She was most pleased to attend to this handsome guest. He possessed a rare combination of dapper sophistication and magnetism, which the fairer sex found hard to resist.

Although he exuded an air of confident arrogance, she thought it only made him appear even more charming. Nonetheless, at the same time, she also felt frustrated by his utter disregard for her presence in the room, addicted as she was to male attention and admiration.

Unlike other men, this man's eyes remained glued to his laptop screen regardless of a beautiful young woman like her in the room.

He took a brief break, but only to claim his cup of tea. He had now switched on the TV and, very much like the last two days started watching a biz show hosted by a stunningly beautiful TV anchor by the name of Rachel.

His eyes took up a special gleam with renewed shine as he watched the charming anchor. He seemed bewitched by the wit and beauty of Rachel; only to make the room attendant feel so…so very jealous of Rachel. She furtively looked at him as she walked out of the room.

Victor was indeed dangerously obsessed with this twenty-four-year-old TV anchor, never once missing even a single of her telecasts and often watching the replay of her recorded clips until late in the night. Finally, this realisation dawned upon Victor that he could no longer bear the separation from his Rachel and, he must do whatever possible to be with her. He yearned for that moment when she would be sitting beside him, smiling at him lovingly. Therefore, Victor steeled up his resolve to take a sabbatical and leave NYC for New Delhi. But, he also knew that in order to make it possible, he must first complete the investigation of this ongoing case of the mysterious puzzles streaming the internet, follow it with the preparation of the closure file of the case and then only he could fly to New Delhi.

Nevertheless, Victor smiled as he dreamt of that beautiful day. The thought of reuniting with his loved ones filled Victor with zeal to work harder… to complete his assignment before the anticipated time. If things moved according to his plan then he would finally be able to go back home after two long decades. Actually, he had been away from home and family for nearly twenty years due to the demands of his duties as a spy, working for the country's security. During these two decades in the world of espionage, Victor had given exceptional services to his country as an intelligence officer working with India's foreign intelligence agency.

However, after so many years of this constant roller coaster ride in the chaotic world of espionage, Victor now felt jaded. He just desperately wanted to go home to spend New Year's Eve with his loved ones. This was not merely a wish but his hidden personal mission. Ah, alas...but little did Victor know about the evil vengeful forces and their hideous plans to hurt his family members! These dark forces had already set out on the ugly mission to destroy Victor's family and his loved ones. If only Victor could get to know about them and reach home in time to save his loved ones!

CHAPTER TWO
THE PRYING EYE

Somewhere in the heart of Lutyens Delhi, a shadowy figure delved deep into the pages of a classified document. He was studying the highly confidential file of an Indian intelligence officer known in the espionage world as Code Pi.

The file detailed the incredible man 'Victor' behind the cover of Code Pi; a dedicated Intelligence officer, a covert operator, a secret agent involved in highly secretive assignments aimed at safeguarding the country's security.

The highly confidential file in the hands of the shadowy figure, chronicled Victor's various missions...only briefly though for reasons understandable.

The file records showed that Victor had forayed into the world of espionage two decades ago as a trade representative in a European country. Under this inconspicuous cover, Victor had tracked down several radical terror groups that operated with the ulterior motive of destabilizing global peace and economy.

Over a span of two decades, Victor's illustrious career as a spy had led him to execute critical espionage activities under an array of false identities.

Victor had also worked briefly as consular official in the various embassies, meticulously gathering visa and passport information crucial for curbing cross-border infiltration and terrorist activities.

As his career progressed, his journey led him from one assignment to the next, each more sensitive and complex than the last.

He went on missions that required him to take up various garbs. As per the demands of the situation, he was sometimes a journalist, a Businessman at the other. There were also occasions when he assumed the role of researcher cum academician or even an artist.

Undeniably, in the world of espionage, Victor held a reputation that was nothing short of legendary, earning the respect and awe of his peers. Due to the record success of the missions headed by him, Victor was a greatly sought-after 'agent Pi', not only by the Indian Intelligence Agency but other top Intelligence agencies worldwide. They sought to collaborate with him in missions against global terrorism.

Indeed, Victor's life and journey had been all about unparalleled dedication and unyielding commitment to the call of duty as an intelligence officer ensuring the security of his country. But it was a hard fact and a sheer truth that this had been possible only at the cost of abandoning a perfect elite life, a loving family, such that anybody would have cherished.

Now, however, after spending years navigating the unpredictable world of espionage, Victor was getting weary of it's ceaseless twists and turns. The endless adrenalin rush, the constant turbulence, once exhilarating, now felt like a relentless storm battering his spirit. He felt jaded and all that he desired was the peace and solace of home. He wanted to go home.

Well, this was indicative of burnout and indeed was a matter of concern that required the attention of the Intelligence Agency. They must address this issue of burnout urgently. It's no understatement, but a matter of fact that burnout continues to be a major factor leading to defection and deflection by the spies. The Intelligence Agency must provide Victor with a much-needed break, a proper compensation and a befitting reward/award. These measures would act like a balm for Victor's weary body and soul, help him get over the tiredness and, charge up his batteries so that he can resume his duties with greater energy and zeal.

Of course, this matter of concern had gotten into the knowledge of the Intelligence Agency and they were keen to come to the aid of ailing Victor with a suitable offer. However, the shocking fact was that, the shadowy figure who was prying into the files had also come to learn about it but contrastingly he wished only for the despicable...and was greatly opposed to the idea of providing any kind of relief or compensation to Victor. Well, as matter of fact, appallingly, this shadowy figure desired just the opposite of the measures needed! He wanted that Victor should defect and he was contemplating as to how.

He firmly believed that there were ways by which Victor could be lured into defection, and it needed to be explored. At all costs, he wanted Victor's name to tarnish, and his reputation to vanquish. Victor needed to be finished off completely and ploy was ready to come into action. The ploy to honey-trap Victor and lure him into committing treason must set going.

"The world must get ready to be shocked by Victor, a traitor and a monster. However, if in case the plan failed to give the desired result and Victor couldn't be lured into the mala fide designs aimed at turning him into a defector, then he must meet a tragic end".

"At any cost, Victor should not return to Delhi and assume the chair of Directorship of the Academy",

Shadowy figure vowed to himself.

The news about the government's decision to summon Victor to the headquarters in Delhi was abuzz in higher circles. Victor's name had been shortlisted for promotion and he was set to assume the directorship of the DIA (Daksha Intelligence Academy), a newly formed wing of the Intelligence Agency. The DIA would be responsible for strategising and bringing about the needed paradigm shift in the modus operandi of the current Intelligence system of the country by embracing the fast-paced Artificial Intelligence.

However, the shadowy figure was opposed to the idea and strongly believed that it would be an act of great injustice if the Government assigned this coveted position to Victor. Obviously, something needed to be done in order to stall this process and, for this, a ploy must come into action, urgently! Victor must meet his doom. Time was running out. Therefore, preparations for Doomsday must invariably start now!!

CHAPTER THREE
BRIEF ENCOUNTER AMIDST MADNESS

It was a bright September morning with a clear blue sky. Butterflies fluttered gracefully over the daisies, and zinnia lining the roadsides in this part of Delhi. Bees hummed and darted playfully among the stunning hyacinths and lilies along the walkways.

But unmindful of nature's beauty unfolding around, 'Rachel', a woman in her twenty-something, looking absolutely gorgeous in her hugging little black Chanel dress hurriedly walked down the street, making her way towards the metro station. The street was rugged and marked with potholes; it's black-top gritty and strewn with loose gravel, yet the young lady navigated the street with adeptness and elegance. That too in spite of her six-inches, high-heeled stilettos.

Even though unaccustomed to walking this kind of road, her sexy pair of long-toned shapely legs with their supple pink feet ensnared in posh Gianvito Rossi pumps plodded and plowed over the rough uneven surface with admirable finesse and precision. She truly presented a vibrant picture of sophistication and grace matching that of a movie star… much to the delight of the passersby!

The metro station was teeming with people, all rushing towards their destination. It was office hours and as such, the station was crowded and chaotic. Soon the train pulled into the station. Rachel, feeling slightly overwhelmed and claustrophobic, reluctantly stepped onto it.

However, soon after boarding, Rachel's apprehension quickly gave way to relief. The compartment was spacious and clean. Rachel inspected her surroundings and noticed an empty seat at just about seven feet from where she now stood. A well-dressed fine young man in a sharp tuxedo seated next to the empty seat caught her attention.

"Was he not overdressed for a metro ride?"

She thought to herself. However, regardless of that queer young man, she decided to take the vacant seat beside him.

She made her way towards that seat, her gaze focused on the man in the tuxedo... and that man, he suddenly looked in her direction; their eyes locking for a moment. Those eyes of his were gleaming with zest for life and, radiated a friendly warmth.

He was the most attractive, damn good-looking guy with distinct fine features. The ever-so-carefree smile lighting up his face was enough to attract people to him; and seemingly, he was having the time of his life, making good use of his assets. His joyfulness was just too contagious.

Unknowingly a smile escaped across Rachel's face. That man in tuxedo was quick to detect this gossamer of a smile on Rachel's face and he instantly reciprocated with a picture perfect brimming, beaming smile. Rachel's heart missed a beat!

"Gosh, he is too handsome", Rachel thought.

The train had now pulled away from the station, and the sudden jolt as it moved forward caused Rachel to lose her balance. Although, she tried to grasp the rails for support but missed it by inches. So much to her dismay, she stumbled and fell on someone seated by the doorway.

She landed on the person's lap, her glasses flying off her head. The passenger upon whom she landed was startled and let out a long gasp. Rachel was petrified with embarrassment but somehow soon enough, she managed to spring up to her feet.

She turned around to say sorry to the passenger. He was a Gentleman in his fifties...and his face...it struck her as a very familiar one. But, at the moment she couldn't register who he was. She politely apologized for causing him inconvenience.

RACHEL: *"Oh, I'm so sorry! Did I hurt you? I should have been more careful."*

The Gentleman, having regained his composure by now and realizing the innocuous turn of events, gave her a reassuring look and replied... *"I am OK!"*

With that, he held out her glasses towards her, retrieving it from the floor of the coach where it had fallen. His voice sounded too familiar to her, but she couldn't quite place him at the moment.

RACHEL: *"Thank you so much, sir!"*

The kind Gentleman smiled back at her and then turned his face towards the window to enjoy the scene outside.

Strangely enough, Rachel somehow felt a strong connection with this Gentleman. She preferred to continue standing next to him, holding on to the rail. She repeatedly stole multiple glances at the Gentleman trying to fit him in her memory's book of acquaintances. But in spite of her best efforts his identity still eluded her.

Minutes later the Gentleman looked up at her and spoke to her with a smile, offering her his seat...

"Please be seated."

He requested as he got up and beaconed her to settle down in his seat. At this particular instance, as his voice reached Rachel's ears the second time, it suddenly struck her ...this fine gentleman was none other than Udai, popular anchor of a television prime time news channel!

RACHEL: (seemingly excited) *"You are Udai sir, if I'm not mistaken!"*

The Gentleman nodded in affirmation to her question.

Rachel felt greatly excited with her discovery. In a mix of exhilaration and sense of euphoria, she drew a quick gasp and pinched herself in order to make sure she was not dreaming. Her heart pounded with anticipation and she began, her voice tinged with awe...

RACHEL: *"Udai sir, I've been watching you on TV for years and I am so happy to meet you face to face. I simply love your shows, your style of anchoring; it's nothing short of captivating. You are awesome!"*

Udai leaned towards her, a warm smile lighting up his face.

UDAI: *"Thank You, I appreciate your kind words. It's always a pleasure to meet someone who enjoys my work."*

Rachel was determined to start a deeper conversation and to gain some wisdom from one of the masters of the craft.

RACHEL: *"Sir, I've been missing your shows... it's been off air for three months I guess!"*

UDAI: *"Well, I've been busy working on a documentary film for the BBC which required me to do lots of research and travel. By the way, young lady, please introduce yourself..., what's your name?"*

RACHEL: *"Sir, I'm Rachel. I work for a recently launched channel, 'Tej' as an anchor, though it's only been two months and I often wonder how I'll succeed in making a mark in this field."*

UDAI: *"Ah, the path to success is never easy but if you truly love what you do and stay committed to honing your skills, the journey becomes an exhilarating adventure."*

His voice sounded velvety smooth like a night breeze on a moonlit beach. He added...

"I think you are a talented lady and you will do exceedingly well in your life and career."

He then swiftly retrieved a sleek white card from his pocket and held it towards her.

"Here's my visiting card in case you feel the need to catch up with me sometime. My station is here, so I must take your leave, bye Rachel!"

Rachel, surprised took his card and held it firmly clasped with her fingers. In her excitement, she could think of uttering only two simple words,

"Thank you!"

She saw Udai get off from the coach, onto the platform. He was soon out of sight lost in the swarm of commuters.

Rachel was feeling quite exhilarated by this brief encounter. Little did she know how this was going to change her life...for good or for bad...only time would tell!

She had no inkling about the second identity of this Gentleman, 'Udai'...that of an Undercover-agent with the country's top Intelligence Agency, who was currently operating in and around Lutyens Delhi, the ever-smoldering cauldron of the highest echelon of political power. Was she going to repent this encounter or be grateful for it, would eventually unfold with time.

CHAPTER FOUR
THE INNOCENT ACQUAINTANCE

Rachel's mind was still caught-up in a whirlwind of emotion and excitement, even after several minutes of the chance encounter with Udai. Actually, she herself had not anticipated that she would be so terribly distraught over the abrupt ending of the interesting conversation with Udai.

Anyway, as for now Rachel was nicely settled in the seat that Mr. Udai had been occupying a few moments ago and she looked outside the window. It was going to be an hour's ride to her destination.

As if reminded of something Rachel purposefully dug into her handbag and took out a book. She adjusted her glasses. Being an avid reader, she always carried a book and preferred to lose herself between the lines and pages whenever she got a chance to. She quickly immersed herself in the book and drifted into her private island, unmindful of everything and everyone around.

Rachel was unaware of the fact that the young man in tuxedo who had earlier caught her attention, had taken fancy to her. He had been observing her with keen interest all the while, his gaze never once leaving sight of her. No, wonder why!

She was a well-endowed stunning young woman with ideal features and proportions to make men's hearts faint and women swoon. Her delicate facial features, thick silky hair, rosy lips and a slim waist that denied the existence of actual human organs undoubtedly made her look gorgeous.

She was so breathtakingly beautiful; men frequently flirted with her and made amorous advances. However, she was indifferent to their advances, as these men had failed to impress her.

Interestingly though, despite her being cold and distant towards them... almost an ice maiden; nevertheless, such was her charm that men were still very happy just to be around her!

Mihir, the man in tuxedo, being young and single, was no exception; his gaze remained fixated upon this woman of ethereal beauty and undeniable elegance, her features illuminated by the soft glow of overhead lights.

However, it was not just her appearance that captivated him but also the book she held in her hands...a novel that bore his name on its cover. This beautiful woman was engrossed in the pages of his debut novel. Her name, he would later come to know, was Rachel. But at that moment, she was a mere stranger, yet a stranger he yearned to know. She was lost in the words of his novel, her eyes dancing across the sentences, her lips occasionally curling into a smile oblivious to the world around her.

As the metro zipped through tunnels, Mihir's mind churned out possibilities to bridge the gap between them, to know the person who held in her hands a novel authored by none other than he himself. Mihir needed a way to connect, a reason to start a conversation. He couldn't let this moment slip away, couldn't allow fate to keep their paths separate. And, so, with each passing station, his desperation to forge a connection with Rachel grew stronger.

A plan, soon enough formed in his mind, a plan woven with the threads of chance and curiosity. He knew he had to seize the opportunity, even if it meant orchestrating a seemingly random encounter. Soon the metro came to a halt. Mihir's heartbeat quickened as he watched Rachel gather her belongings and move towards the door, the novel still clutched delicately in her hands. This was his moment, so making a quick decision, he too, disembarked at the same station and steeled himself for the encounter that was about to take place. He moved towards her, holding out a metro card, and gave a gentle tap on her shoulder.

"Excuse me," he said, his voice laced with a gentle charm as he touched her shoulder. "I believe this metro-card dropped off from your mobile case."

Rachel looked at the card, a puzzled expression on her face.

"Oh, really? ...Thank you,"

She replied, her voice soft yet uncertain. She glanced at her mobile case, doubting that the card could have slipped out unnoticed.

Mihir's lips curved into a disarming smile.

"Apologies for the intrusion," he said smoothly. "I couldn't help but notice that you are reading a novel that I happened to have authored. I'm Mihir."

Rachel's surprise was evident in her eyes as they met his. .

"You're the author? I...I had no idea."

A spark of discovering a shared secret flickered in her eyes.

"It's always a delight to meet someone owning and enjoying a copy of my novel,"

Mihir said his words genuine and warm.

"May I ask your thoughts on the book so far?"

They began walking together towards the station's exit. Rachel's eyes held a twinkle of interest.

"I must say, your writing has drawn me in completely. The characters are so vivid, and I'm truly intrigued by the plot. I'm only a few chapters in, but I can hardly put it down."

Mihir's heart swelled with a mix of pride and joy.

"I'm truly grateful to hear that. If you ever wish to discuss any part of the book, please don't hesitate to reach out. My email is mentioned on the bottom end of the backside cover page of the novel."

As they stepped out onto the platform, their connection seemed to have deepened. Rachel's face was beaming with a radiant smile.

"I'll definitely keep that in mind. I'm Rachel, and thank you again for returning the metro card."

Mihir chuckled softly, his eyes holding hers for a moment longer.

"Feels good to be of some help to you dear Rachel!"

Rachel, amused by Mihir's rizzing ways and pretentious claim of returning her metro-card, burst into laughter. She had known it all along that her metro card had not fallen and had actually been with her all the time. Here was yet another man trying hard to get close to her. But there was something about him that drew her towards him. She liked him. Her laughter echoed through the space between them as she responded flirtatiously,

"Mihir, have a great day and I must say it has been a pleasure knowing you."

Mihir's gaze held hers, an unspoken understanding passing between them.

"It's been a great pleasure too meeting you Rachel."

Rachel smiled a touch of mystery in her eyes.

"Mr. Author, may I request you to please pen down an author's note on my copy of your novel. This reader will be more than happy,"

Rachel's voice was soft and imploring.

Mihir pleased with the request enthusiastically did as asked. Then bidding each other good-bye, they parted ways, but not without a sense of anticipation.

As Rachel walked towards her office, she couldn't help but feel a sort of excitement and intrigue still lingering on after the chance encounter. Little did she know that this seemingly innocent acquaintance would be the beginning of an unexpected friendship and a series of delightful interactions around shared interest in literature, life and everything in between.

CHAPTER FIVE
CONSPIRACY OF THE ASTRAL-VENUS PLEXUS

Mihir, a talented, young business graduate from Cornell had come to Delhi from NYC in pursuit of his passion. He was here in a quest to capture the essence of Old Delhi on the silver screen. He sought to unravel the multiple layers of history, culture and tradition that wove themselves in the fabric of this city. He wanted to bring the stories of its resilient inhabitants to life through the lens of his camera.

Mihir loved Delhi, as it was here that he had spent the first sixteen years of his life. He was born and brought up in a joint family based in Greater Kailash, Delhi. His dad belonged to a Delhi based business class family, living in a joint family in their Greater Kailash house, back then in 1960s until later part of 1980s. In 1981 when Mihir was in his sixteen, a big misfortune struck the family. The family business suffered huge losses forcing them to sell off their GK house to pay off the debts. The family then moved over to Gurgaon to their ancestral Farmhouse built over a plot of mixed-use land. Mihir's father, taking inspiration from his entrepreneur father-in-law, went on to set up a pharmaceutical company named Atharva, on his share of the land.

Lady Luck smiled on Mihir's dad and Atharva Pharmaceutical Company flourished, making good turnover, and generating decent profits that kept multiplying over the years. Mihir flew off to States for undergrads from Penn State; and then followed it up with a graduate degree in Business Management from Cornell. However, Mihir had always nurtured a hidden desire for filmmaking and when he evinced his interest in seriously pursuing a degree in filmmaking, his parents supported his passion. So, soon after graduating from Cornell, he joined the prestigious New

York Academy of Film-making, where he mastered the art. The academy was a melting pot of talent, ideas, and culture. At NYFA, he learned the craft of filmmaking from the stalwarts in the field.

Then and there ignited in him a burning desire to explore the unexplored, to document the stories that hadn't been told as yet and in midst of this self- discovery he was drawn to Delhi, his home town, from New York after years.

During the first two days after landing in Delhi from New York, Mihir simply roamed and explored the narrow, bustling lanes of Old Delhi. He was entranced by the sights sounds and smells that surrounded him. The chaotic Chandni Chowk market with it's labyrinthine rows of shops, the aromatic street food stalls, the centuries-old architecture...all made for a perfect set for this filmmaker's dream project. But he knew, his vision required more than just beautiful visuals; it demanded an understanding of the people who had lived in this maze of history.

This morning, Mihir had started early from his parent's mansion in Gurgaon for Mandi House in Connaught Place., But his car got caught in the midst of a traffic jam caused by unexpected road blocks due to some ongoing agitation. The agitators gathered in great numbers had barricaded the highway, pressing for their demands from the government.

Mihir found himself stranded, unable to move his car even an inch in the gridlocked traffic. All his attempts to steer his car out of the jam were futile. Now the only option left for reaching the destination was taking the Delhi Metro Rail Service. So Mihir abandoned his car and set off to take refuge in the Delhi Metro, the lifeline of the city. He reluctantly joined the swarm of commuters heading on foot towards the Delhi Metro, a place he had not visited in years.

Rachel too was out in her chauffeur driven car this morning, en` route to the recording studio in CP. She also had to face a similar predicament, forcing her to leave her car in the very same traffic jam in which Mihir's car was trapped. Just like Mihir, she too had to opt for the metro. Ultimately, Rachel and Mihir both found themselves boarding the same metro; their paths intersecting by play of destiny... clearly the working of the Astral, Venus and Cupid plexus.

They could, have easily forgotten their simple acquaintance due to this chance meeting, but destiny had other plans. In spite of their busy schedule, they decide to meet again, the very next day. Initially, they met over a cup of coffee, to share stories and dreams. As the days turned into weeks, their meetings only got longer and became very much a part of the daily routine. So, it didn't take long and a genuine friendship blossomed between the two.

In the heart of Connaught Place, they started to meet for lunch daily, their conversations stretching into the late hours. Their friendship burgeoned into romance. The Indian Arts Place, the historical ethnic gems and art shop in CP became their favorite haunt where they spent hours admiring the artworks. Also, Mihir bought priceless little gifts for his lady love from there

It was during one of these rendezvous, Rachel's perceptive eyes once again spotted Udai sir, the media personality whom she had encountered while commuting in metro just few days back.

Udai was there in the shop looking for some genuine sapphire stone to make a ring for himself. Rachel walked up to him and started a conversation with him. She was pleasantly surprised to realize that Udai remembered her name. This serendipitous encounter led to the forming of a new friendship between the trio- Rachel, Mihir, and Udai and they then onwards kept meeting often. They found in each other not just friends, but kindred spirits, drawn together by their shared passion and dream for creating something great and exceptional.

Soon, a collaboration formed between them; Udai with his knack for crafting compelling narratives, Mihir with his cinematographic skills and Rachel with her dynamism, together conceptualize a collaborative project...a short art or documentary film that would weave together their individual stories, skill sets and dreams.

However, they knew their dream project required an anvil...and the search for this anvil led them to Hazel, a historian and educationist of countrywide acclaim. Incidentally, this person Hazel was none other than Rachel's own mom. But, even Rachel was unsure whether her mom Hazel would take an interest in their collaborative project?

CHAPTER SIX
THE RETRO JOURNEY WITH HAZEL

It was indeed a lovely romantic evening in the capital city today! Clouds were floating wantonly over Delhi skies, catching evening sunlight to give romantic purple, golden and pink hue to the dusk. The weather was just perfect for going out on a leisurely stroll around the city streets and parks.

Hazel had in fact, just returned home from the spa of the neighbouring shopping arcade and she looked out from the window of her quaint Bohemian quarter located in the secluded corner of the sprawling green university campus. The lush green carpet of grass in the lawn below seemed to beacon Hazel, inviting her within it's fold. Hazel just loved the simple joys in the lap of nature like no one else, and she unfailingly spent an hour daily tending to her plants in the garden. To be in love with nature like Hazel, one must have faced many ordeals and setbacks in life just like her. One must have walked through fire, faced hurt and betrayal at the hands of mortals just like her; for it is only then that one can truly learn to fully appreciate the nurturing beauty of nature. Because only and only then can one truly experience the invigorating feel of green grass under the bare feet and the magic of colorful tapestry of sky overhead.

This evening, Hazel took notice that a certain kind of balmy quietude hung in the air. The leaves and boroughs of the trees in the compound below bore a solemn appearance. The glistening water of the lake too seemed engaged in a silent secret conversation with the air; like young lovers. Everything appeared cool, serene, calm and placid... in fact, each element of nature seemed steeped in a silent meditation. Could it be the hush and quietness before the ensuing storm?

Hazel had just returned home this evening after a relaxing session at Aura Thai Spa. This Spa was one of her happy places where she felt rejuvenated to cope with the midlife crisis, the accompanying body pain, thinning hairline, aching joints and hot flashes. Hazel was an academician by profession, whose charm and intellect, equally captivating, graced the hallowed halls of Delhi Women's College as Professor and head of the department of History. She was a pillar of wisdom and inspiration for young minds.

Well, however, on this particular evening after returning from the spa, Hazel didn't somehow feel restored. She felt lazy and lay ensconced in the comfort of her rocking chair by the window, her family album placed on her lap. It's true, there comes a time when you are bound to slow down, especially when you are in your post fifties; because now time ceases to fly, it glides. Actually, it even sits by your side and talks to you. And that was exactly the kind of rendezvous Hazel braced herself for this evening.

As she turned the sepia-tinged pages of the album and flipped the photos one by one, she found herself drawn to the past. Two particular photographs stood out...the frozen moments of the past, the cherished memories.

Her fingers gently caressed one of the photographs. This pic, she remembered so well, had been clicked in Manali during her early college days some twenty-seven years back in 1994. She had been on this hiking trip along with other student members of the trekking club of her college; and that also included the college heartthrob, Richard. All the girls of the college had crush on him but Richard had given his heart away to Hazel. Both Richard and Hazel were madly in love with each- other.

The picture that Hazel held in her hand transported her to that beautiful day at Zero Point in Manali. Lo, here she was sitting on the pillion seat behind Richard, nestled close against him on his bike. She had wrapped her arms around his waist, her body pressed against his; while Richard, with his wind-swept hair and that irresistible smile of his (that always made her heart race) flashed a victory sign.

Their journey on bike from Manali, across the winding roads of Rohtang Pass to beautiful Spiti Valley had been more than an adventure; it was a magical whirlwind...a dance of passion and laughter against a backdrop of snow-kissed mountains.

As he drove, Richard shouted over the roar of the engine,

"This is freedom!"

Rachel smiled, knowing true freedom for her was the feeling of Richard's heartbeat against hers, the rush of wind that tangled her hair with his, and the heat of their entwined bodies cutting through the mountain chill.

Richard revved up the engine, and they rode at top speed weaving around potholes and past lumbering yaks. The thrill of speeding was a testament to their youthful energy and zeal. Stealing glances at each other with eyes that sparkled with excitement and a deeper, unspoken promise Richard kept driving.

Every stop during the journey brought moments of stolen kisses, each one more lingering than the last. The kisses deep and intense tasted of adventure and desire, making the frigid air around them feel like a midsummer breeze.

By the time they reached Zero point, they were breathless...not from the altitude but from the intensity of shared passion that engulfed them.

She knew then in her heart that it didn't matter if their next journey took them to the end of the earth, as long as they were together, every road led to paradise. Both Richard and Hazel knew they were made for each other and, they vowed to be partners for life. It was a silent vow though. They could read each other's silence. Their hearts beat in sync, their eyes spoke to each other louder than words.

A smile lit up Hazel's face as she relived those moments through the photograph. She let out a sigh and picked up the other photograph. This particular picture taken exactly twenty years ago depicted her small family encircled by friends.

As her eyes settled on that photograph, a kind of magic unfolded, whisking Hazel to that very day the picture had been taken. Hazel found herself transported back to that moment, a participant and an observer simultaneously. In her mind's eye the scene unfolded like a film projected on the canvas.........There she was, a stunning Hazel in her later part of the twenties, along with her husband Richard, a dashing young officer and their adorable four-years old daughter Rachel. They were basking in the golden sunlight on the enchanting beaches of Goa. The sound of crashing waves and the soft sand beneath their feet added to their joyous mood.

They had gathered for a sundowner at Calangute beach along with their school and college friends, Phil, Luis, Regina, and Angela, to celebrate Richard's recent promotion and his transfer to the beautiful coastal town of Candolim in North Goa.

PHIL (raising his glass): *"To Richard, the rising star of our group! Congratulations on the promotion and beginning of the exciting new chapter in Goa"!*

The friends clinked their glasses together, exchanging laughter and well wishes. The children giggled as they built sandcastles nearby.

RICHARD (smiling) *"Thank you, Phil. I couldn't have achieved this without the support of my lovely wife, Hazel, who has stood by me through thick and thin".*

Hazel blushed, her eyes filled with pride and love for this handsome man who has been her lover since college days and subsequently her husband of five years of marriage till date.

LUIS (teasingly): *"Well, Richard, I hope this promotion doesn't make you too busy to forget us. You'll still come and hang out with us, ordinary mortals, right"?*

RICHARD (laughing): *"Of course, Luis! We'll always find time for our old gang".*

REGINA (sipping her drink): *"I must say, Richard, you getting posted in Goa is like a dream come true for you and Hazel! You guys had fallen in love with Goa during the college trip six years back, and you dreamed about settling down here. Finally, your dream has come true"!*

HAZEL (raising her voice slightly): *"God has been greatly kind to us and I'm really thankful"!*

Under the evening sun, the group of friends decide to engage in a friendly game of beach volleyball. The sand beneath their feet felt warm and comforting as they formed teams, laughing and joking with each other. With laughter and banter filling the air, the friends split into two teams. The game began with great enthusiasm. The competitive spirit that had once fueled their college days came alive once again on the sandy shores of Goa.

The ball flew back and forth, and the shouts of encouragement and taunts filled the air.

Between serves and volleys, the players took breaks, catching their breath and reminisced about the wonderful time they had spent at Stevens College in New Delhi, their alma mater.

Richard had earned his Master's degree in Statistics from Stevens College. He also found Hazel, the love of his life here in the campus itself. Hazel was pursuing a master's in History from the same college.

As the game reached its peak, Richard's athletic prowess shone through. With lightning-quick reflexes and precise shots, he led his team to victory, much as he did during their college days.

REGINA (panting, playfully): *"Richard, you're on fire! It's like you never left the court! You could have been a basketball player in the national team".*

RICHARD (laughing): *"Well, basketball is fun, but I'm happy with my job in civil services. It's the perfect balance for me".*

After the game, as the sun began its descent into the sea, casting a golden hue over the beach, they gathered around a bonfire, their hearts brimming with nostalgia and warmth. They shared stories of their school and college adventures, the victories and defeats, and the friendships that were forged. Each memory was a treasure, reminding them of the bonds they had formed at Stevens, and how those bonds had endured through the time.

LITTLE RACHEL (excitedly): *"Mommy, Daddy, look at my sandcastle! It's so big"!*

The friends turned their attention to little Rachel's sand castle, marveling at her creativity and, also at the cuteness of this sweet little girl. She had inherited the beauty genes from her ravishingly beautiful mom and handsome dad.

ANGELA (playfully): *"Rachel, that's so grand and beautiful, you're a really creative! I see a bright future ahead for you. What do you want to be when you grow up"?*

Having blurted this question Angela wasn't really expecting any answer from a four years old kid. But to everyone's surprise Rachel promptly replied ....

RACHEL: *"I want to be a superhero and save the world."*

ANGELA: *"Wow, that's a great aspiration dear Rachel! Bravo!"*

RACHEL: *"But I also want to be a princess and live in a magical castle!"*

At this reply everyone but couldn't control the rush of laughter and heartfelt admiration. Their eyes sparkled with delight, and their hearts swooned with affection for the little dreamer before them. They were all momentarily transported back to their own innocent childhood days, to a time when the world was filled with endless possibilities and boundless joy. An overwhelming sense of warmth and nostalgia washed over them as they reminisced about their own childhood days. The golden hues of the sunset painted the sky as a gentle breeze swayed the palm trees.

The evening turned into night. The group continued to revel in their celebration, singing the songs they had once learnt from their very sweet and talented music teacher during the music-class, back in their school Days. Rachel and other children were amazed by their parent's childlike wantonness. Never before, they had seen their parents so joyful and uninhibited. They too joined them in singing their favorite songs. They danced and sang under the starry sky, their laughter carried by the ocean breeze. It was a night of joy, camaraderie, and dreams that stretched as far as the horizon. Little did they know that this reunion would be the first and last one of many cherished memories they would create in the land of sun, sand, and endless possibilities.

CHAPTER SEVEN
CHALLENGES FROM THE MAFIA

As Hazel flipped through the photos of the album, it stirred afresh the vivid memories of those days with Richard... those early days when they were in the process of settling down in the government-provided accommodation in Goa. They used to excitedly, explore the neighbourhood and local marketplace during the weekends, getting new stuff for furnishing their accommodation, making it cozy and comfortable for their loving daughter, Rachel.

Rachel then used to be such an adorable sweet kid. She had taken after her dad by way of looks and sporty disposition. Doting Hazel was so glad about it. She simply adored her husband, Richard, an honest administrative officer who worked diligently in the government offices. He was a man of integrity, devoted to his duty and committed to making a difference in the lives of the people he served.

However, Richard's noble aspirations came at a cost. The government-provided accommodation where he must live with his beautiful wife Hazel, and their daughter Rachel, was located in an area with poor roads and infrastructure. Nevertheless, it was a fairly picturesque coastal town of north Goa, but the lack of good schools nearby added to Hazel's struggles as she tried to provide a nurturing environment for Rachel.

Richard's demanding job often kept him away from home for long hours, leaving Hazel alone to manage the household. Hazel's problems and worries deepened as the monsoon season rolled in, bringing with it relentless rain and cloudbursts. The torrential downpours wreaked havoc on the roads, making commuting a challenge, while prolonged power cuts added to the family's frustrations.

But it wasn't just the forces of nature that troubled Hazel and Richard. The shadowy underbelly of Goa, consisting of mining and drug mafias, cast a menacing presence. Goa being a mineral rich state, mining of iron, bauxite and manganese ores had been going on legally and illegally since the mid-20th century and had emerged over the years as a central component of the state's economy.

The illegal mining community was very affluent, powerful and nefarious running a parallel black money economy. The mindless mining activity by them was posing a big challenge to the health of Goa's economy and ecology. More so, the recent China boom that had driven iron ore prices to rocket sky high was accompanied by a mad rush of miners in Goa to extract everything and send it to China. This caused rampant increase in Illegal mining particularly peaking around the latter half of 2000, coinciding with the time-period when Richard took up charge as a civil services officer in North Goa.

As Richard settled into his new role, he discovered a tangled web of corruption involving mining, drug, and sand mafia, operating with impunity. Richard was quick to analyze the whole scenario and realized that the situation was alarming and, that he was required to take quick action. Dedicated as he was to uprooting corruption, he started targeting the illegal activities that plagued the region unmindful of warnings from the mafia. He waged a relentless fight against corruption with unwavering commitment, enraging the mafias. Richard was shocked when he witnessed the huge scale of devastation to environment and ecology brought about by Illegal mining. It had butchered Goa's entire hinterland, destroying paddy fields, forests and water resources, besides causing irreparable damage to local wildlife. An astounding 850 million tonnes of mud and mining waste had accumulated all over the mining belt. The waste lay in the form of huge hills composed of clay and toxic metals that cascaded down into Mandvi and Zuari rivers along with heavy downpours during the monsoon.

Richard, being an environmentalist to the core, got together with the local environmentalists and NGOs to file a petition in court against uncontrolled mining. He succeeded in bringing about court orders banning all illegal mining operations. And subsequently the dumping activity too came to an end with the end of illegal mining.

Mines that run illegally were all closed down and as such a large community of miners in Goa were very frustrated. They were out of jobs and rendered cash-stripped, so were the truckers and transporters who used to be engaged in transporting the produce and waste of mining activity.

The mining mafia and the drug mafia were driven into a frenzy due to the loss of business, and they then connived with local goons to create unrest by misleading the unemployed masses. As such, there was an upsurge in civil unrest. People were resorting to anarchy, taking law into their own hands and things were headed for worse. The mining mafia had strongly warned Richard of dire consequences for coming in the way of their illicit operations, creating an atmosphere of fear and apprehension.

Hazel was aware of the whole scenario, and it constantly troubled her peace of mind. She kept worrying for Richard's safety. One stormy night, as rain poured relentlessly, Hazel sat by the window, anxiously waiting for Richard to return. The flickering candlelight cast eerie shadows on the walls, heightening her unease. Finally, the front door creaked open, and Richard stepped inside, soaked to the bone.

HAZEL (worried): *"Richard, you are wet all over! Here bend down a little so that I can dab out your wet hair with the towel. I'm so relieved you're home. It's been a dreadful day. Power's been out for hours, and the rain shows no sign of stopping".*

RICHARD (gently touching Hazel's cheek): *"I'm here, Hazel. Don't worry. We'll get through this together".*

Their conversation was interrupted by a loud crash of thunder, rattling the windows. Hazel's fear intensified, knowing that their predicament wasn't just about the weather.

HAZEL (hesitant): *"Richard, we've been through so much since we came to Goa. Do you think we made a mistake by standing up against those criminals"?*

RICHARD (resolute): *"No, Hazel. We've done the right thing. I won't let fear dictate our lives. We're fighting for a better future, not just for us but for everyone... Rachel too".*

As Richard held Hazel close, they found solace in each other's arms. Their love and determination fueled their resolve to face the challenges that lay ahead.

CHAPTER EIGHT
THE PIQUE SELECTION

Days turned into weeks, and the monsoon's fury gradually subsided. Richard continued his fight against corruption, undeterred by the threats that loomed over him. Hazel, ever supportive, managed to find a glimmer of hope amidst the darkness.

In the year that followed, Richard's relentless pursuit of the drive against corruption made a lasting impact on Goa's governance. The town began to flourish, it's people rejoicing in the positive changes brought about by Richard's efforts.

However, the mafias of Goa were seething with frustration. Their empires once invincible, had crumbled under the relentless pursuit of Richard. He had been a thorn in their side for too long, and they were determined to remove him from their path once and for all. Little did they know that a new force too was watching over Richard – the government itself.

As the mafias tightened their grip around Richard, the government too clandestinely increased the level of security around Richard. While keeping it a guarded secret from Richard, who was unaware of it, they kept a constant vigil on Richard.

Ever since Richard got posted in Goa, the government had been taking note of his extraordinary capabilities and unparalleled achievements. Improving Goa's governance in such a short span was no less than a feat, and they were impressed by Richard's unwavering dedication to duty. His relentless spirit for fighting corruption and his ability to outmaneuver the most cunning criminals made him a valuable asset. Government saw him as a formidable force against organized crimes and decided to induct him into India's elite intelligence agency, the IA.

As a matter of fact, Richard had been an outstanding candidate ever since his training days at LBS Academy of Administration in Mussoorie. Besides academic excellence, he had been equally good in extracurricular activities including sports, particularly adventure sports like rock climbing, river rafting, and paragliding that require extraordinary skill, stamina and endurance. The then-serving Director of the academy had shortlisted his name and placed it on the list of officers with great potential. Now, after observing Richard's exceptional accomplishments in Goa, they were very sure that Richard was the perfect candidate for induction into India's elite intelligence agency.. As such, secret agents had been deployed to discreetly monitor Richard's movements and associations, in view of the impending danger that Richard faced from the mafias.

Richard was topping on the hit list of mafias due to his tough stand against them in Goa. So, without losing any time, concerned Intelligence agents approach Richard, to inform him about the impending dangers and also about his selection into the country's top intelligence. Beyond doubt, Richard was taken by total surprise, and was overwhelmed with a deep sense of honor on learning about his selection.

CHAPTER NINE
MISSION UNFOLDS

It was past midnight and drizzling incessantly in the month of October. The campus of Richard's government quarter in Goa was shroud in an eerie mist, illuminated only by the soft glow of the moon. There had been a power outage all through the day and hadn't been restored yet, however the drizzle cast a glistening sheen to the whole panorama.

The tall Crocodile bark trees and Malabar Kino trees in the compound swayed gently in the breeze, their leaves whispering secrets to the night. October rain had brought a chill to the air, and the secluded government quarter seemed like an island in itself.

Here, under the cover of darkness, four shadowy figures moved with the stealth and grace of panthers through the campus, their movements deliberate and purposeful. These figures approached the boundary wall of the courtyard. The wall was wet and slippery with overgrowth of moss following months of incessant rain. Undeterred, the four shadowy figures scaled the wall with the dexterity of a mountain cat and silently made their way across the courtyard to the backdoor that opened into the main building.

A slight push on the door, and they were inside the house. Apparently, the door had been left unlocked, as if with the intention of allowing hassle free entry to the intruders.

These intruders, however, were no ordinary men; they were officials and agents of top intelligence agency; whom Richard and Rachel had been awaiting.

Under the cover of night, the secret agents had assembled for a clandestine meeting with Richard and Hazel. Among them, Alvin distinctly stood out, a charismatic and intelligent Intelligence official who had transitioned from the armed forces. Alvin's experience, acquired during his service in the armed forces had molded him into a master tactician and he took the charge of explaining the mission's intricacies to Richard.

Alvin's voice was laced with the authority born of experience as he spoke to Richard. His words were as precise as his actions, and he had an uncanny ability to mold and convince even the most skeptical minds to follow his plan of action, no matter how daunting the odds.

Alvin: (Speaking to Richard, his tone hushed, measured yet urgent) *"Richard, we are meeting to discuss a secret mission. This Top Secret mission is of utmost importance.*

Your unwavering dedication, capabilities and accomplishments as a civil servant have brought you into the notice of the highest office. Based on your unique set of skills, integrity and expertise you've been chosen for a mission that will test your mettle like never before.

We need you to serve our country in a more covert capacity. This requires you to disappear from the public eye, to become someone else entirely. The very essence of who you are will be concealed for the greater good.

You will undergo necessary training and then, sent offshore with a new identity to track down the masterminds behind the terror attacks throughout the country.

Your mission is to dismantle their network and bring them before the court of law. The operation is highly sensitive, also risky and could endanger Hazel and Rachel. So this mission entails sacrificing normal family life and marital bliss"

Richard listened intently, a deep furrow forming on his brow. He absorbed the gravity of the situation, fully aware that the path Alvin described was fraught with peril. He loved his wife and daughter dearly, even more than his own life.

Richard found himself in a great dilemma, caught amidst the chaos of the covert mission, the dangerous world of mafias and the ensuing separation from his family. But Richard was not the one to be easily deterred from duty.

He knew that the sacrifices were necessary to protect his family and ensure the success of the mission he had been entrusted with. He was aware of the fact that already the mafias had joined hands, making the threat to his loved ones even more real; and soon afterwards with Richard's covert mission intensifying, the dangers surrounding his family would be more ominous.

Richard knew he had to keep them safe, and he must take a heart wrenching decision. It was a painful proposition, but the one that would ensure the safety of his family. Richard finally steeled up his resolve as he looked into Alvin's eyes, and he took the most agonizing decision – one that would tear his family apart.

RICHARD (In unwavering voice): *"Alvin, I've always been dedicated to my country. I'm ready, I'll do whatever it takes to serve our country and protect my family."*

Alvin nodded approvingly, knowing that Richard possessed the unwavering resolve required for the mission. As the conversation further unfolded, Hazel's presence couldn't be ignored. Alvin was aware of the difficult conversation that lay ahead.

ALVIN (Turning to Hazel, his voice softer now) : *"Hazel, for the safety of both you and Rachel, we strongly advise that you file for divorce. Richard's life is in constant danger due to the enemies he's made in the course of his duty. This mission will further put you both in grave danger, and any connection to Richard must be severed in the eyes of the world. It's the only way to keep you and Rachel safe. Your safety and Rachel's future are paramount and we can't afford any loose ends."*

Hazel's eyes widened in shock and disbelief. She couldn't fathom the idea of divorcing the man she loved. Tears welled up in Hazel's eyes as she grappled with the shocking suggestion of divorce. The weight of the situation bore down on her like a leaden cloak, and for the first time, she felt the full gravity of the mission's implications.

HAZEL (Desperately, In a protesting tone): *"But Alvin, we can find another way. I just can't end my marriage like this. Divorce? How could you suggest this? Richard can be discreet. We'll move, change our identities if needed. But we can't end our marriage!"*

Alvin maintained his composure and steady gaze, understanding the turmoil in Hazel's heart. He had seen countless families torn apart by the ruthless world of espionage.

ALVIN (In soft and gentle voice smooth as silk, but resolute): *"Hazel, it's the only way to protect you and your daughter from the dangers that loom. We are not asking you to end your relationship; we just need you to file for divorce on paper, to ensure your safety from the mafias. It's a measure to divert their attention from you and your daughter. The criminals will not hesitate to target you, being Richard's wife and use your love against you. By appearing unattached, you'll be less vulnerable. A divorce would provide a cover, keep you out of harm's way, and allow Richard to carry out his mission effectively. Your safety and Rachel's future are paramount. We can't afford any loose ends. It's a sacrifice, but it's one that is necessary. This is the harsh reality we face."*

Hazel's resistance was palpable, but Alvin's arguments were unyielding, his words a blend of persuasion and conviction. Alvin's ability to sway decisions was unmatched, and he left just no stone unturned in making Hazel understand the dire need for divorce. Hazel, however still appeared shocked and saddened with the turn of events. It was a difficult decision, and she struggled to get to terms with the heart-wrenching move that was expected of her.

That rainy night, after the Intelligence officials left, Richard sat Hazel down, the dimly lit bedroom casting long shadows across his face. He held Hazel's hand in his and looked into her eyes with an imploring gaze.

RICHARD: *"Hazel, we need to talk. The situation has escalated beyond what we can handle and we are at a point of no return. We must work according to the plans of the Intelligence Agency."*

Hazel's eyes welled up with tears as she struggled to comprehend the magnitude of what Richard was saying.

HAZEL: "But Richard, we are a family. How can we be apart? Divorce is not the answer."

RICHARD: "Hazel I don't want this any more than you do. But our love for Rachel and each other should guide us. Divorce in this case, is not about ending our love, but protecting it. It's about creating a safer environment for Rachel to grow up in. This is the only way to protect Rachel and ensure her future."

Hazel wiped away her tears, her gaze wavering as she spoke.

HAZEL: "I understand, Richard. Rachel means the world to us, and we need to do what's best for her. But can we really keep our love intact through a divorce? I fear it will bring more pain.

Richard reached out, taking Hazel in his embrace, his face bearing a sad look, his voice filled with conviction."

RICHARD: "Hazel our love is stronger than any piece of paper. Divorce won't change that. We will find a way to stay connected, to support each other through this. Our love will endure, even if we're physically apart."

Hazel looked into his intense eyes. Richard nodded and smiled. Hazel smiled back, a glimmer of hope shining through her tears.

RICHARD: "Our bond is unbreakable. We will always be a family no matter what. I will do everything in my power to keep you both safe. And, I believe in you Hazel. You are my strength, my whole world. You have so much talent and potential. Once you are back in Delhi, I want you to resume your career as a lecturer at the university. You deserve to follow your dreams too. This will also ensure Rachel's upbringing in the best environment and in a good company."

Hazel's eyes sparkled with a newfound determination as she embraced Richard's words. Her initial shock and sadness, her reluctance to work upon the plan of the Intelligence Agency was getting transformed into a new found purpose.

After all she was a woman of intelligence, strength and logic. She realized the necessity of the charade for the safety of her family and the greater good. It was a role she must embrace for the sake of her loved ones and the country.

She, being a capable woman, was now ready for the mission. Intelligence Agency had assured her facilitations for resuming the lectureship at the college in Delhi University, the position she had been holding prior to shifting to Goa. Besides, she was also assured with help of added financial support to provide for a comfortable life.

HAZEL: "If you think so Richard, there must be a good reason behind it and your trust in me has given me renewed strength. Yes, you are right Richard. Our bond is unbreakable. If this is what it takes to protect Rachel and ensure her future, then I'm willing to do whatever it takes. We'll always be a family, no matter what. I'll make you proud, and Rachel will grow up knowing that her parents made sacrifices for her safety and happiness."

Richard smiled; relief and gratitude washing over him.

They now sat in close embrace, acutely aware that their time together was fleeting. The weight of their impending separation hung in the air, but so did the desire to make these moments of togetherness unforgettable.

Their eyes locked, filled with longing and devotion, their hands entwined, fingers tracing lines of each other's face. Their lips met in a kiss, a silent promise of love. In the subtle intimacy of that night, they found solace in each other's arms, cherishing the love that would sustain them in the days to come. As the night wore on, their whispers filled the room, sharing dreams and hopes for the future. Each word was a promise, a commitment to return to each other, no matter what.

CHAPTER TEN
CLANDESTINE ESCAPADE

The following day dawned at Richard's household with a sense of solemnity in the air. It was a lovely morning. A joyous chorus of birds singing and chirping resonated in the air with the promise of a perfect Sunday. The sky stretched overhead in a brilliant shade of azure blue. Gentle strokes of stratus cloud formation were dotted all across the blue canvas, resembling white, fluffy, delicate puffs of Dandelions. It reminded one of the childhood days when children would rush to catch the white Dandelion puffs floating in the air. They would then, while holding it in their hands, close their eyes, make a wish, and blow the seeds into the air. No one knows for sure how or why people started making wishes on Dandelions.

However, Richard and Hazel both were too busy this idyllic Sunday morning, preparing for the challenges that lay ahead. The mission of Intelligence Agency was going to test their resolve and redefine their identities.

In the world of espionage, the fate of the families lay uncertain as the lines between truth and deception blurred. It entailed enduring separation, heartache, and the burden of secrets. However, the couple understood the importance of their role in the grand mission of the Intelligence Agency.

Executing upon the plan, the couple along with little Rachel drove down in the car to a quaint church in Panjim, in the heart of Goa. It was a place where the echoes of prayers had resonated for generations.

As they stepped inside the church, the hushed reverence enveloped them. Sunlight streamed through the tinted glass windows, casting warm, ethereal glow upon the faithful. Hazel and Richard knelt in quiet contemplation as they prayed for strength, courage, and protection in the uncertain future that lay before them.

They waited there expecting a meeting with the IA agents but there was no sign of them. They came out of the church, clicked a few family pictures and then set forth on the journey ahead. They were heading for the next destination according to the plans of IA, the Mangeshi (Lord Shiva) Temple, nestled amidst the lush greenery of Priol, twenty-two kilometres from Panjim. Drive to the temple was like a short pleasure trip.

Mangeshi Temple was a sanctuary of peace and spirituality, a place where devotees sought solace and blessings. It is believed that the deity here granted the wishes of the devotees if it were made with good intentions. It was a breathtakingly beautiful, 450 year old temple with elegant facade in hues of blue, gold and white.

There standing before the majestic deity, the couple bowed their heads in reverence and sought his blessings and protection. They awaited the IA agents to approach them here but still there was no sign of them so they moved on to the next destination slotted for the meeting.

Their journey now headed towards Shantadurga temple in Kavelum, at about 30 kilometers from Panaji located on the slope of foothills of a mountain chain. It was a scenic drive into the world of natural beauty and tranquility along gently winding roads. The trip offered panoramic views of the surrounding countryside, glimpses of beautiful traditional Goan houses with red tiled roofs standing amidst coconut groves.

Little Rachel, too, was excited and she enjoyed the view of the lush green fields and swaying palms. The locals could be seen going about with their daily routines, tending to farms or engaging in friendly conversations by the roadside. As they drove further closer to Western Ghats, the scenic foothills became even more captivating with thicker foliage.

When they entered the main temple premises, they were greeted by sewaks who offered them vibrant colored silk saree and dhoti which devotees are required to wrap around themselves, symbolizing purity, reverence and humility. The temple priest led them with a dignified grace through the temple's inner sanctum, where sounds of bells and chants reverberated, creating an atmosphere of profound serenity.

But Richard and his family were destined for an even more immersive experience. Due to the high ranking government position of Richard, they were granted special access to the most sacred room within the temple, a privilege reserved for the very few. This room, the inner sanctum was dimly lit with the soft glow of earthen lamps casting dancing shadows upon carvings on the wall. Here in this sacred chamber, the main deity resided. As Richard and Hazel bowed before the deity, the priest bestowed upon them special blessings. It was a moment of deep spiritual connection, a communion between the earthly and the divine.

However, unbeknownst to all but a select few, here the IA officials discreetly waited in the shadows of the inner sanctum, along-with look-alikes of Richard and Hazel, draped in sari and dhoti similar to Richard and Hazel. A masterful plan with lookalikes of Richard and Hazel was about to be orchestrated. As the priest conducted the ritual, the look-alikes of Richard and his family seamlessly assumed the roles of Richard and Hazel, and with a practiced finesse they exited the temple and got into Richard's car after the completion of the rituals. To any common observer, they were indistinguishable from the real family.

In the meantime, actual Richard along with his family got whisked away in secrecy by the IA officials to a secure secret spot. There the IA officials made a chilling revelation to Richard; the mafias had planted a bomb in Richard's car with the clear intent of taking his life and the lives of his loved ones. Therefore, the IA had orchestrated upon the plan to deceive the mafia by placing Richard and Hazel's lookalike in the car. The idea was to mislead the mafia into believing that Richard and his family perished in the car blast.

The plan worked and just as the IA had desired, the mafia were actually deceived into believing that Richard and his family had met with their tragic end with the bomb blast. Waves of euphoria engulfed the mafia and big celebration ensued with the kingpins getting careless with their ways. The police, fully prepared was waiting for this moment and they launched a timely surprise attack on the gang, succeeding in arresting the mafia dons.

The second phase of the plan was now in action. In the shadows of the night, IA officials sneaked Richard and his family out from Goa and took them to Delhi. Soon after reaching Delhi, Hazel seamlessly transitioned into her role as a lecturer in the college, a position she had to give up after getting married to Richard. Richard's job in civil services got him postings in far-flung places outside of Delhi so Hazel had to discontinue her job to accompany Richard.

For Hazel and Rachel, going back to life in Delhi offered a semblance of normalcy in stark contrast to Goa, where danger lurked in every corner for them. Rachel, bright eyed and eager to explore, was more than happy with the exciting life in the big city. She joined a reputed school and went to school in school bus with great enthusiasm. She was making new friends and getting popular with all.

CHAPTER ELEVEN
THE FINAL GOODBYE

The IA's plan was in motion, each step being perfectly executed with meticulous care. That day too finally arrived when Richard was to say goodbye to the most precious ones in his life…Hazel and Rachel.

A turbulent storm of emotion swirled within the hearts of Richard and Hazel…love, longing, despair and hope all churning up at the same time. Hazel stood by the doorstep, her eyes glistening with unshed tears. The radiant smile on her face was a façade, concealing the pain of separation that gnawed at her heart.

Little Rachel clung to her mother, her small arms wrapped tightly around Hazel's waist, as if sensing the impending void that Richard's absence would create. Richard stood before them, his strong exterior betraying none of the turmoil inside. His gaze lingered on Hazel, the love of his life, and Rachel, the daughter he cherished above everything else. His heart ached with the knowledge that he couldn't share the entire truth with them, couldn't tell them all about the dangerous path he was about to tread.

"I promise I'll be back soon,"

he said, his voice tinged with an emotion he couldn't name.

"Take care of each other, and never forget how much I love you both."

Rachel, albeit too small to understand the complex affairs of the adult world, but nevertheless, sensing a foreboding intuitively, now clung to her father's leg, her innocent eyes searching his face, as if trying to memorize every detail.

Hazel's smile wavered, and teardrops escaped the corner of her eyes. Richard leaned down, carried Rachel up in his arms and held her close to his heart. He then drew Hazel closer to his chest into a deep embrace. He kissed them softly on forehead and cheeks as if to say goodbye… because his voice was choking and would not come out. He then released them from the embrace, turned and walked away drawn by a profound sense of duty, his heart heavy but his resolve unshaken.

At that moment, little did Rachel and Hazel realize they were not going to see Richard for decades to come.

Richard, with a profound sense of duty set off for training as a spy to the Institute of Intelligence Agency, a secretive facility hidden from plain sight, known only to those initiated into the world of espionage. Here he was required to undergo a transformation, shedding his former identity to become a formidable spy.

Hazel was presuming that Richard would come to meet her and Rachel after a year or two, at the end of the training period, but sadly enough the wait turned out to be an unending one. Twenty years had gone by, and Richard never returned.

Only occasionally, though, Hazel and Rachel received letters from Richard, but astonishingly, these letters worked like magic potions for them. It gave them the wings of hope that kept them flying aloft and provided them with the strength to soar like eagles.

Remarkable, as it was, Richard's letters were most of the times addressed to his daughter, and they usually carried anecdotes from his childhood or growing up days. However surely enough, in a subtle manner the letter echoed Richard's love for Rachel and Hazel. Interestingly, these letters reached Hazel's mailbox in neat bundles only once every four or five months and they were not handwritten but typed. The letters also didn't divulge about the whereabouts or other current personal details of Richard.

It was only obvious these letters were reaching in edited form probably after scrutiny by the IA. These letters were neatly stacked inside a sealed envelope and dropped secretly in their mailbox next to the main door by an unknown somebody.

Nevertheless, Hazel and Rachel were very grateful for these letters…these were like a savior and lifeline for the daughter and mother duo, and they clung to the memories of the man they both loved, the letters being the bridge that connected them. They would sit by the window place, reading and rereading his letters, each word in the letter a testament to their enduring love. The letters were a source of hope and courage for both of them and their love for Richard remained unwavering despite so many years. His absence was a constant ache in their hearts, and the letters were a balm. They hoped that one day, their family would reunite, and the shadows that separated them would finally dissipate.

CHAPTER TWELVE
RACHEL'S ASCENT

Hazel, sat alone, still lost in thoughts, surrounded by the old photographs that held memories of a life she once shared with Richard, evoking bittersweet emotions in her. In the midst of the nostalgia, she failed to notice that the purple evening sky had turned deep, velvety black, with countless twinkling, diamond-like stars. The moon, a golden crescent cast a gentle glow over everything.

It was the incessant buzzing, the sounding of the familiar ring of her mobile phone, that pulled Hazel out of her reverie, back into the present. Hazel reached for her phone, the caller ID displayed Rachel's name. She answered the call, her voice a soothing melody.

"Hello, my sweet, Rachel."

From the other end of the line, Rachel's nightingale-like chirpy voice reached Hazel's eardrums, cheering her up.

"Hi, Mom. I just left the office, and I'll be home in about an hour.

Do I need to pick up your thyroid medication on the way?

Also we are having two surprise guests for dinner but you need not worry about cooking as I've already ordered the food. It will be delivered in time. I've done the payment so just relax and chill till I get home."

Hazel's heart swelled with pride and love for her daughter. Rachel had grown into a responsible, caring young woman, shouldering the responsibilities of their household as well as office. Hazel gazed out of the window to behold the moon; she couldn't help but smile. Rachel was her anchor, her guiding star, a beacon of hope and love in the darkness of their shared loss.

Hazel admired her daughter, Rachel greatly. Rachel had defied all odds and soared to considerable heights in the world of media, creating a niche for herself in this very competitive field. She had made it so far and so well, only by dint of her determination, ambition, and an unyielding spirit that mirrored the strength of her father, Richard.

Rachel had graduated with honors in Economics from the very prestigious Delhi College of Economics, a testament in itself to her intelligence and dedication. Despite getting campus placement... tempting offers from Multinational corporations that promised wealth and prestige, she turned them all down. These high-paying jobs required her to move to the United States and she opted to remain in Delhi, close to her beloved mother. It was a conscious choice driven by love for her mother and also by her secret desire to become a media personality in the world of Indian television.

From a very early age, Rachel had been attracted by the allure of showbiz. So, right after graduating from college she started looking for opportunities to work with the media. Her dreams took to flight when she was chosen as a newsreader after auditions by a newly launched TV channel. So she got drawn into the world of television as a newsreader, her voice resonating with confidence and authority, making her very popular with the viewers. But destiny had greater plans for her.

Rachel's talent, beauty and charisma, caught the attention of industry insiders... producers and directors both. Soon, offers from various channels started pouring in for her. These were offers for hosting business talk shows and shows on wealth management...that required her to provide investment and financial planning advice. Rachel soon found herself at the helm of many such shows, dispensing investment and financial advice to a captivated audience.

Hazel had always been a guiding force, a constant source of strength for her daughter in her journey towards shaping her dreams. Hazel admired her daughter's determination and willpower. She was most courageous too, always smiling sweetly even in face of adversity. People and the cameras both loved Rachel's sweet smile.

For Rachel, being in front of the camera was more than just a career; it was a way to connect with her absent father. Rachel believed that her father might be watching her on television, wherever he was in this world, and she wanted to make him happy with her smile. She wanted him to take pride in her for what she had become.

Yes, during those moments before the camera's gaze, Rachel couldn't help but wonder if her father, the man she loved the most, and whom she had missed each day for two decades, was watching her from some distant corner of the world. Her father's eyes, if they were on her, would see his daughter become a confident, successful woman that he can be proud of as a father.

Rachel took great care about her appearance before each show, dressing up with elegance and sophistication just like her father. To ensure that he recognized her, she wore a particular, delicate gold chain with a unique pendant bearing the initial 'R', a cherished gift from her dad on her fourth birthday.

As Rachel continued her ascent in the world of media, she did so with the hope that one day her family would reunite. Hazel too eagerly waited for that day to dawn and she no longer felt trapped by fear. She had the satisfaction of witnessing her daughter, Rachel grow into a strong and confident young woman, inspired by the unwavering determination of her mom and dad.

CHAPTER THIRTEEN
THE NINE UNKNOWN MEN AND MARC

Marc sat comfortably by the window of the plush Pallazio Hotel suite, a glass of Champagne Shake in hand. He gazed at the urban expanse beyond, savoring the cityscape that unfolded. The hotel room, adorned with tasteful opulence, basked in the soft glow of twilight. The strains of Mozart's finest piece of symphony drifted through the air. Marc relished in the indulgence, a rich creamy mix of Moet Imperial with lychee liqueur and vanilla ice cream, his all time favorite.

Marc was a man of considerable wealth and was a connoisseur of vast acclaim. He was an Indian multi-billionaire entrepreneur, the executive chairperson and founder of Atharvaa Bio Pharmaceuticals Limited. It was the fastest-growing Indian pharmaceutical company engaged in developing, manufacturing and marketing biopharmaceutical products globally, having a presence in over fifty countries.

The company's global success was a testament to Marc's strategic acumen and visionary leadership, yet his identity extended far beyond the boardroom.

Marc was married to Athira, the only single child of her parents. Athira's dad was the founder and owner of Lubik Pharmaceuticals, a drug-manufacturing company based in Gurugram. Athira, being the only child of her parents, was the sole heiress to Lubik Pharmaceuticals.

Marc's marriage to Athira was more than a union of hearts. For both Marc and Athira, their marriage was the convergence of wealth, a partnership marked by ambition. Marc's marriage was symbolic of the duality he lived... holding on to a public persona of an executive chairperson and a perfect family man at the same time. But beneath it, he had a hidden existence as a member of a secret society, Illuminav, the Indian Illuminati, originally known as 'The Nine Unknown Men'.

This secret society held ancient wisdom and modern power in its grasp, its origin and influence woven into the fabric of history. As the legend goes, this society probably was founded in 273 BC by emperor Ashoka of India after the bloody war of Kalinga that took the lives of 100,000 million men.

As we all know, Ashoka was deeply affected by the bloodshed and immense loss of lives caused by the Kalinga war and he renounced the path of senseless violence, converting to Buddhism. He took an oath that his rule would henceforth be peaceful; the pursuit of Dharma being the most significant aspect. A covert community was presumably founded by the name of, 'The Nine Unknown Men', consisting of nine brilliant men deemed worthy of entrusting with the task of realising Ashoka's dream of forming an Utopia, a land of peace ruled by Dharma.

These nine men were responsible for collecting and preserving all the knowledge available in the empire at the time. They were guardians of scientific, philosophical and political knowledge and were responsible for overlooking the task of erecting several rock edicts across the length and breadth of the country with principles of Dharma written on them.

If in any case a member of this society wished to retire for any reason, he would first choose a worthy successor to this lineage. Thus, this coveted society remained active and kept burgeoning discreetly, contrary to the general assumption that it had ceased to exist. In the modern times, this society had come to be known as Illuminav; with people like Marc, taking upon themselves the onus of carrying on this beautiful legacy.

Marc however wasn't confined to Illuminav only but was a man of many interests that transcended the corporate world and the secret society. He was also an art collector, the finest connoisseur and patron of art and literature. Nevertheless his passion was not limited to buying new art and heritage artifacts, but even extended to reclaiming the old stolen ones…only to return them to their rightful places within India. This mission was not just a personal endeavor, but it was a pledge to preserve the nation's past for future generations.

However, right now his primary focus was on deciphering the scriptures and cryptic codes contained in the ancient book of scriptures gifted to him by the old priest of an ancient temple in Uttarakhand.

Marc had stumbled upon this ancient rock temple this summer while trekking in the thick alpine forests of the Garhwal region of the Himalayas. The temple dated back to the times of Pandavas, while the book, (basically a bundle of well-preserved handwritten tamrapatras securely bound together) belonged to the same period or even earlier. The priest entrusted this invaluable book to Marc as he intuitively felt that Marc was the right man with whom the book would remain safe. Also, he felt that Marc had the capabilities and resources to decipher the scriptures and cryptic codes in it. This book held the secret to change the world forever, the priest believed, and he had strong faith that Marc would enlighten himself and the whole world with the revelations from this book.

The music of the symphony continued to waft through the room as Marc adjusted his cufflinks, his thoughts now lingering on the meeting that lay ahead. He was delighted at the prospect of rendezvous with the genius who had decoded all the intricate puzzles posted by him on the internet. This man he was going to meet had to be a genuine polymath as he had accomplished the most challenging feat; finding the elusive solution to his impregnable puzzles.

Marc reflected on the series of events he had anonymously set into motion, the last month. The thirty days gone by had seen him posting, one after the other every week five intricate puzzles on the web, inviting all the netizens to provide solutions to the puzzles.

He kept track of those enthusiasts who attempted and solved the puzzles. This effort was a part of his plan to search for a genius who could help him in deciphering the book of scriptures. Only a few netizens were able to solve three or four of his puzzles, and just one man...could solve all the five. Now Marc sought to get this man as his ally as he was a genius who could help him in deciphering the book of scriptures.

Marc was eagerly looking forward to meet the brilliant man who held a mind that was a mirror to his own, a mind that matched his own and a mind that he sought to ally. The city lights continued their luminous ballet outside the window as Marc pondered upon the ensuing meeting set to take place in his suite in few hours.

Meanwhile, not very far from him, in the same city, Victor, the genius whom Marc awaited, was leisurely relaxing in a bathtub. The bathtub was filled with lukewarm water to which essential-oils of sandalwood, lavender, and rose had been lavishly added along with aura cleansing salt mix. This was Victor's much-deserved relaxing and rejuvenating aromatherapy after spending several restless days and nights relentlessly working to solve the puzzles and finally succeeding.

After half an hour, Victor, now fresh out from the bath, soon immersed himself in yogic meditation. Ever since his training days at the Intelligence Academy, Kundalini practice, soul control Ninja and Tibetan Tumo had been an integral part of his routine and helped him remain focused and calm as he carried out the daily affairs that were of no ordinary man's calling.

Victor's every single day at work demanded highest level of genius combined with the versatility of an actor. He was required to possess the astute-ness of a cold-hearted logical strategist along with the agility and tenacity of an acrobat. Needless, to say Victor did posess all the required attributes and exercised them with self-consuming devotion for duty based upon unconditional love for his country.

With another half an hour gone by, Victor, having completed the meditation session, now switched on the TV to watch the latest episode of his favorite 'Rachel's show'. His face lit up with the glow of a thousand bulbs, and his eyes gleamed with interest, widening as they focused on the beautiful, enchanting face of Rachel flashing on the TV screen.

As he watched the show, he proceeded with his lunch, seated on the floor with legs folded. His lunch today consisted of an Italian platter…a plateful of rich Mediterranean salad, a bowl of steaming Tuscan Portobello Stew, along with a side dish of flavorful Sweet Potato Panzanella.

After he was done with his lunch, he sat down before his laptop, streaming through the latest posts of Rachel on social media; a compulsive act, almost an addiction. He attentively watched the recent podcasts and videos of Rachel as he dressed up to leave for the meeting that was scheduled at nearby Pallazio Hotel. Dusk had settled in, and the urban panorama had transformed into a tapestry of twinkling city lights. Victor stepped out from his hotel and proceeded towards the suit 7007 of Plazzio for the meeting.

CHAPTER FOURTEEN
THE MEETING OF GENIUS MINDS

In the dimly lit suite at the Pallazio Hotel, Marc readied himself for a crucial rendezvous in his hotel suite. As he looked at himself in the mirror, it reflected the image of a man with refined taste; a someone who had always prided himself for his sartorial elegance. His tailored suit exuded an air of sophistication, every detail done with precision.

Soon he heard the distinct knock on the door he had been waiting for. With a measured stride, he approached the doorway. As he opened the door, he stood tall and confident, exuding an air of quiet authority; his keen eyes assessing the man on the other side.

Before him on the other side of the doorway stood Victor, a man equally distinguished in his appearance. Just like Marc, Victor's attire too was impeccable, a testament to his good taste. He looked impressive with his eyes bearing the sharpness of a man of intellect. In that fleeting moment, both men made observations that would have escaped the notice of the common man. Victor immediately recognized the man in front of him but he didn't make it obvious.

As the eyes of the two men met, a silent understanding passed between them. It was a recognition that they were not ordinary individuals but men of discernment, each with a story to tell and a mission to fulfill.

"Good evening,"

Marc greeted, extending a hand in welcome.

"Good evening,"

Victor replied, accepting the gesture.

As they moved to the seating area, Marc offered a drink, a gesture of hospitality. They settled into the plush chairs, the ambience steeped in an aura of intrigue and purpose.

"My name is Marc,"

he began, his tone measured.

"I'm the VP of Atharva Pharmaceuticals."

"Victor."

Came the response, equally measured.

"I'm a researcher and data scientist"

The conversations flowed, each man revealing just enough to convey their respective roles and backgrounds. Marc, with a sense of gravity, began to unveil the mission that had brought them together.

"Victor," Marc began, his voice carrying the weight of their mission *"I've recently come into possession of an ancient book of scriptures from India. It holds secret codes and cryptic messages that I believe are of profound significance and could alter the course of history. I need you to decipher these codes, to reveal the knowledge that has remained hidden for centuries."*

Victor looked at Marc with a fixed gaze, trying to understand the task at hand, though still not sure of its exact purpose. Still he nodded at Marc affirmatively and spoke with determination.

"Wow, it sounds interesting! This is a quest for knowledge and seems very exciting, I'm ready to embark on it. I won't let you down, Marc."

Needless, to say both Marc and Victor seemed intrigued by each other's enigmatic persona. However, Marc had certain gnawing doubts.

"How was it possible that Victor, a man of such evident genius, diverse knowledge, immense talent and extraordinary demeanor be simply a data scientist and researcher? There had to be more to Victor than what meets the eye."

As for Victor, he too could sense that there were layers to Marc, secrets behind his refined exterior.

Amongst the two men, Marc decided to take the first step towards forging deeper ties. He extended an invitation to Victor with earnestness in his voice.

"Victor I invite you along with your family for lunch at my new holiday home on Roosevelt Island this Saturday if you are free. Me myself and my wife would be greatly pleased."

The offer steeped in courtesy was a gesture of hospitality, but it concealed a deeper motive. Marc was determined to uncover more truth about Victor, to understand the man behind the mask.

Victor, equally intrigued by Marc's hidden depths, accepted the invitation.

"Thanks a lot for the invitation, Marc. I'm looking forward to the Saturday and will surely come with my wife and my daughter."

Victor was aware that this lunch could be an opportunity to unravel the enigma, Marc.

Both of the men were playing games, each harboring secrets, and neither willing to reveal their full identities just yet.

CHAPTER FIFTEEN
BIG BETRAYAL FROM THE BRUTAL HEART

At Hazel's house, an air of anticipation was very much palpable this evening. Rachel and Hazel were busy making last minute dinner preparations for the guests expected to arrive any moment now. Both of them were dressed elegantly and in great style to welcome their guests, Udai and Mihir.

The placement on the dining table was tastefully laid for the special dinner, adorned with gourmet Mughlai delights and fine wine, flanked by exotic chinaware and crystal glasses. Tonight's dinner was an occasion to discuss more than mundane topics like good food, weather, and air quality of Delhi. It was about convergence of interests, passions and opportunities.

The guests arrived, and the evening unfolded with lively discussions about their shared passion. They chatted with delight and laughed at each other's jokes as they savored Mohabbat-ka-sherbat, Rachel's handmade specialty made of sugar syrup and rose petals from the organic roses that bloomed in their own garden. Hazel then served them rich Hyderabadi biryani with Rogan Josh and Shish kebab to delight their taste buds. Lively conversations continued as they savored each course and sipped wine in between.

Udai, with his penchant for history, Mihir, with his budding filmmaking aspirations, both had gathered at Hazel's elegant home to seek Hazel's insight and her guidance for their filmmaking project. They were keen to embark on an ambitious project...the making of a short film encapsulating the essence, rich history, and culture of Old Delhi in a manner not done before. Well, what better guide could there be for this than Professor Hazel with her profound understanding of history. She could prove to be an invaluable asset. Both men were eager to collaborate with Hazel and Rachel for this project. They aspired to create a masterpiece, worthy of screening at the prestigious Cannes Film Festival under the category of art cinema. Making such an extraordinary movie required fusion of their individual talents and unique stories.

This project was conceptualised by Mihir while he was still in Manhattan pursuing the last semester of filmmaking course at NYFA. Well, luckily enough, Udai, with a keen eye for spotting talent and having a knack for recognizing potential, was quick to gauze Mihir's outstanding capabilities as a great filmmaker. So when Mihir suggested a collaborative filmmaking project, incorporating the fusion of their unique talents and expertise in their respective fields, Udai found the proposal resonating deeply with his own vision, and together they set out on the venture...a mission to preserve and present the vivid stories of the remarkable city, Delhi, through their film.

Hazel too had been lately contemplating harnessing the potential of cinema and television for bringing forth to the world the knowledge about the forgotten facets of Indian history. Mihir's proposed project came as an opportunity that she had been awaiting. It could turn out to be a merger of her academic knowledge with a visually engaging and far-reaching world of cinema for imparting the knowledge and so she gladly accepted the offer to collaborate on the project. The chance to be a part of a team working on a documentary movie with such a rich subject matter was a dream come true.

The gathering around the dinner table had been fruitful. All of them had found common ground, and their vision for the project aligned. They all shared their ideas and insights into how the movie should take shape, and their excitement was palpable. They all felt like they had found kindred spirits who shared their enthusiasm for history, culture and art.

The evening came to a pleasant close, and the men got up and prepared to leave. The men thanked the ladies for a soul-enriching dinner and some great conversation around the table. As they made their way for the main door, Hazel and Rachel followed behind them to see them off. It was a full moon night and as they stood by the doorway, bidding farewell, the cool moonlight washed over them. It had indeed been a wonderful evening, a rare chance for Hazel and Rachel to open up and engage in meaningful conversation with men who shared their passion.

After the departure of the guests, Hazel and Rachel started tidying up the kitchen, chatting about the evening, how wonderful it was to connect with like-minded individuals. Though the men had gone, Hazel and Rachel were feeling overwhelmed with a rush of energy and a feeling of jubilation. The discussion had ignited their passion, and they had glimpsed the potential of their collaboration.

A few minutes later, Mihir's car pulled back into the driveway. He had returned, realizing he'd forgotten his mobile phone. Rachel helped Mihir retrieve the phone and followed him out of the house. She accompanied him along the path to the driveway where his car was parked. This winding path was canopied by beautiful Night Jasmine, Amaltas, and Pilkhan trees. The trees stood like silent sentinels in the moonlit night.

The air outside was cool and carried the sweet, intoxicating fragrance of the flowers. It was soothing to the senses and felt almost heavenly. Rachel and Mihir paused under the Night Jasmine tree, admiring the beauty of the delicate, white flowers that had fallen on the ground below, around their feet.

Breathing in deeply the air filled with fragrance of the flowers, they felt overwhelmed with a desire to savor and prolong this moment of unexplained magic. The moonlight spilled through the flower-laden boroughs of the Golden Shower tree and bathed them in its romantic glow.

The night seemed enchanting and stirred something within them. A strange, romantic tension filled the air...and even before they could realize, they got drawn into each other's arms, their bodies locked together in a tight embrace. Their lips met in an unexpected moment of passion, and the magic was undeniable. For a fleeting moment, the world around them disappeared, leaving only the magic of the night. The pleasure of the intimate kiss that sealed their love was intoxicating and made them breathless.

However, the feeling of being watched compelled them to draw away. Their hearts still pounding with the excitement of the stolen kiss, they reluctantly parted. It took them a few moments to gain composure. Rachel ran her fingers through her hair to set it in place, while Mihir unlocked the door of his car. Waving goodbye to Rachel, Mihir drove off into the night, his face still flushed with intense feeling. Rachel too headed towards the house, flustered due to over racing pulses and increased throbbing of her heart.

Rachel slowly walked towards the house, her heart still racing madly. As she passed by the mailbox, it somehow seemed to beacon her and with rekindled hope she paused by it. She decided to check the mailbox, despite having already checked it in the morning. She put her hands inside the mailbox and to her surprise her fingers actually touched upon some paper in there and she quickly retrieved it. To her immense joy it was an envelope similar to the ones that carried her dad's letters.

It had been two years since they had received any letter from him. Excitement surged through her, and she couldn't contain it. Clutching the envelope tightly, she rushed inside the house to share the news with her mother, her heart filled with anticipation and hope. She was curious about the contents and hoped to soon re-establish communication with her father.

Rachel burst into the house through the main door, envelope clutched in her hands, her face red with excitement. Hazel looked at her through her glasses and could sense Rachel's excitement. Breathless, Rachel exclaimed,

"Mom, you won't believe what I found in the mailbox!"

She showed the envelope to her mom.

The thrill of the unknown painted their faces, an infectious energy passing between mother and daughter. Together, they fumbled with the envelope, hands shaking with eagerness as they ripped it open. The content of the envelope spilled out. There came out a one page typed letter, presumably from Richard and a few more pages with pictures of Richard. Tears of joy brimmed in the eyes of Hazel and Rachel as they saw Richard's face looking at them from the pages. Richard's face still looked so handsome, actually more alluring and magnetic than before. He was one of those men who grew more attractive with age... aging like wine, as people say.

However, Hazel and Rachel's elation was short-lived and soon turned into shock and disbelief as they looked at the whole picture. The shockwave hit them with full force. Richard was not alone in the photographs; two beautiful women accompanied him. One of them appeared barely in her twenties.

Richard, surrounded by the two women, looked content and blissful. The trio in the photograph looked like a happy family, at comfort and ease with each other, exuding warmth. The other photograph revealed him alongwith the two women in beachwear, enjoying the sun on a pristine white beach; which again seemed like a snapshot of a happy family, having a good time together. Apparently, Richard had embraced a life they could not fathom.

Hazel, with a sense of foreboding, turned her attention back to the letter. The letter's revelation struck like a thunderbolt. The truth, stark and brutal, leaped from the pages. It wasn't a letter from Richard, instead, it was a notice from the Intelligence Agency. Richard,... their Richard, he was charged with defection... labeled a double agent, a traitor. He was accused of compromising national security by leaking classified information to enemies. Criminal charges loomed over him for divulging confidential government information to rival nations.

The shock got further amplified as the letter conveyed a revelation that confirmed their suspicion... Richard had married a foreign spy, a divorcee with a daughter from her previous marriage. They were living together in hiding. The Intelligence Agency, in a stern directive, commanded Hazel and Rachel to sever ties with him and stipulated that in future should Richard attempt any form of communication with Hazel and Rachel they must inform the Intelligence Agency.

The room seemed to spin for Hazel. She was dizzy and felt as if the ground has been pulled from beneath her feet. Grappling for support, she clutched onto a nearby chair. Rachel, her eyes wide with disbelief, tried to comprehend the enormity of the situation. Her father, a traitor? Her heart refused to accept the damning information. She struggled to reconcile with the image of her father as a traitor. The shattered fragments of their world lay strewn before Rachel and Hazel, and the enormity of the betrayal left them grappling with a pain that seemed unsurmountable.

The air hung heavy with a sense of loss and disbelief, as mother and daughter confronted the harsh reality. Heartbroken, they were left to themselves… to pick up the pieces of their shattered trust, to recover from the colossal deception that cut deep into the core of their existence. The foundation of their life had crumbled, leaving behind a void filled with unbearable pain.

CHAPTER SIXTEEN
THE GAME BEGINS

Rachel and Hazel, reeling under the shock of the letter's scandalous revelation seemed drowned in the deep sea of despair. They spent the whole night sitting around the dining table unable to catch even a wink of sleep. Hazel was slumped in the plush chair, tears staining the silk scarf around her cape. The room seemed to echo with the sobs that shook her body, now, then and again. Hazel was too broken and inconsolable.

By the break of day, the air in the room had grown leaden heavy with fatigue and frustration. Tears had dried up leaving its mark on Rachel's cheek as she stared at the empty wall of the room, a turmoil building up within her. Storm of emotions raged... sorrow, despair, and anger all mixed with a growing unease. A sudden surge of fury now coursed through Rachel's veins, and with fierce determination, she snatched the letter from the table along-with the pages carrying the damned pictures, intending to tear them and shred them into pieces. However, pausing for a while she glared at the pages, as if to look at Richard's picture for one last time, before tearing it apart...but her eyes widened in disbelief. The picture was not there! The image that had caused so much agony, had vanished into the thin air! Bewildered, she flipped the page, expecting to find her father's image on the reverse side, but it was blank as well.

Panic clutched at Rachel's heart as she shifted through the pages again and again, hoping for the glimpse of the photographs or the damning notice. Yet, each attempt yielded nothing but empty sheets, devoid of the once incriminating evidence.

The disappearance was uncanny, defying the laws of logic and reason. Rachel's mind, now a whirlwind of doubt and suspicion, questioned the unexplainable disappearance. Of course, the Intelligence Agency surely will not issue notices that disappear into thin air. Was someone orchestrating a sinister plot to tarnish her dad's image? Was this a deliberate attempt to drive a wedge between him and his family. With a sense of urgency, Rachel unfolded about the disappearing act to Hazel.

RACHEL (voice tinged with urgency): *"Mom, I don't understand. The pictures, the notice from the Intelligence Agency, they are gone…disappeared from the pages. Like they never existed".*

Hazel, her eyes still swollen from weeping, tears still rolling down the cheeks, looked up and listened intently to what Rachel was saying, deep concern etching her features.

HAZEL (confused): *"What do you mean? How can pictures just disappear"?*

RACHEL (frustrated): *"I mean, look at this, Mom. (shows the empty pages) Dad's picture, the notice…they're missing, they are gone, vanished".*

HAZEL (examining the empty pages): *"But how is that even possible"?*

RACHEL (with a deep breath): *"I don't know, Mom. But this is not normal. Why would Intelligence Agency issue disappearing notice.. Dad works for the Intelligence Agency, and I can't shake the feeling that there's something more to this. Like someone is trying to weaken him, also turn us against him by showing him in low light. Dad's job with Intelligence Agency must have made him enemies. Mom, someone is toying with us. They want us to doubt Dad, to believe he's involved in something sinister".*

Hazel's eyes widened with a mix of surprise and worry. The room felt charged with unspoken tension as the gravity of the situation sank in.

HAZEL (steadying herself): *"We can't jump to conclusions, Rachel, but I trust your instincts. Now, actually even I'm beginning to suspect a foul play. Surely some sinister game is being played to malign Richard. We can't risk your father's position. We must do something…we need to plan something discreet".*

RACHEL (determined): *"I know, Mom. We have to be careful. Dad's reputation is at stake, and I won't let someone destroy our family".*

As they sat together, mother and daughter, their mind once clouded by grief, now sharpened with a determination to uncover the truth. They decide to unravel the mystery behind the vanishing pictures and notice, to expose the puppeteer pulling the strings in this clandestine drama.

HAZEL (thoughtfully): *"Yes Rachel, we need to get to the bottom of it. For this I think we must revive ties with the old network of Richard and socialize with acquaintances to gather information quietly, but without alerting anyone. We don't know who we can trust. We have to be discreet. We don't want anyone to suspect that we're digging into this".*

RACHEL (nodding): *"Yeah, just like one of Dad's covert operations! I've been thinking the same. The fact that we are dad's family, living here in Delhi, is known only to a few of dad's colleagues in the DIA, and then this suspect too knows about it well enough. Whoever it is, it's trying to manipulate us and I have an intuition that he will contact us soon. And when he does contact, we must act as if we have fallen for his game. He must believe that as intended, we hate Dad for how much he has wronged us, and we are vengeful to the extent of destroying him, if it had been in our power".*

HAZEL (softly): *"We're in this together, Rachel. No matter what comes, we face it as a family".*

The duo, united by a common resolve, decide to turn the tables on the malevolent force that sought to tarnish Richard's reputation. Hazel and Rachel, with newfound determination, plan to track the suspect by reaching out to trusted allies within their social circle, seeking connections and extracting information that might unravel the threads of conspiracy entangling their lives. However, it was pertinent that they must keep their main motive discreet.

As the first ray of dawn painted the sky, Hazel and Rachel totally exhausted by now, their minds consumed with conflicting thoughts and emotions, get startled by the unexpected sounding of the doorbell. Who could it be, so early at six am in the morning? The intrusion at such an early hour sent a ripple of alarm through them.

RACHEL (whispering): *"Mom, keep your phone with recording mode ready. I'll check who it is"*.

Hazel nodded, quickly concealing her phone with a towel turned on the video recording. With caution, Rachel approached the door, her senses heightened in the aftermath of the episode of the night.

As she opened the door, a mix of surprise and confusion washed over her. Udai stood there at the threshold looking very excited, his enthusiasm undiminished by the early hour.

UDAI (apologetic): *"I'm sorry for disturbing you so early, Rachel, Hazel. But this is urgent"*.

Rachel, still grappling with the abrupt and unexpected, managed a polite smile.

Rachel: (curious) *"What's so urgent, Udai"?*

UDAI (excited): *"Today's the last day for registering for an annual conference in NYC... you know, ... for the media people and documentary movie-makers. Only a few hours are left for the deadline...I mean, precisely one hour is all we have to register for it. Mihir has given me special passes for the event, which he managed to get from one of his NYFA alumni association contacts. Altogether, we have three passes for the event. But now firstly we also need to mandatorily register for the event online. So let's do it now. Get your laptop. It's a great opportunity not to be missed out. The Conference will have eminent speakers from the media world, entertainment industry, academia, press and the government. It will be an enriching experience and we will get to do good networking. All three of us are going to attend this prestigious conference"*.

Rachel and Hazel could not keep themselves from catching Udai's contagious excitement. Although the prospects were indeed great and promising Rachel and Hazel still found themselves f caught in a surge of conflicting emotions. On the one hand, the professional opportunity was enticing, but on the other hand the family turmoil revolving around the pressing matter of Richard's predicament lingered in the background. Nonetheless, they acknowledged the importance of the offer.

RACHEL (grateful): *"Thank you, Udai. Let me get my laptop; we can register right away"*.

As Udai and Rachel delved into the task at hand, Hazel couldn't shake off the feeling of lingering unease. The sudden appearance of Udai on the scene raised doubts in her mind. Was Udai the malevolent schemer and culprit?

However, Rachel seemed unperturbed by Udai's presence, so Hazel dismissed the nagging thought. Amidst the chaos of the drama that had unfolded in their household during the night, this unexpected turn... the annual conference thing, emerged as a fleeting opportunity for Rachel and Hazel, providing them a brief respite from the storm that had engulfed their lives.

Hazel headed towards the kitchen to brew some ginger tea for all of them. She was feeling totally exhausted and her mouth felt parched. As she came back with tea and cookies, signs of exhaustion clearly showed in her gait as well and overall demeanor. Lines of worry were etched deep on her face. Udai's keen eyes didn't miss the sign of distress on her face as he reached out for the tea and cookies from the tray she held out.

UDAI (concerned): *"Are you okay? You look a bit off. Is there anything I can do to help? Please let me know"*.

HAZEL (softly and a bit hesitant): *"It's been a challenging night for us , Udai. Some unsettling things have happened. We are dealing with it. But for now, let's focus on this registration process. We'll talk about it later"*.

Udai sensing the gravity of the situation, nodded understandingly. The trio immersed themselves in the online registration process, the urgency of the impending deadline momentarily overshadowing the enigma that had gripped Hazel's household. The flight tickets for New York City were swiftly booked as well.

With the journey to the bustling metropolis imminent, preparations for their departure became the focal point of their day. The thought of escaping the shadows of conspiracy and stepping into the vibrant energy of New York City brought a mix of emotions for both Hazel and Rachel. As they went about packing their essentials and organizing their travel documents, their minds occasionally drifted back to the disturbing letter.

RACHEL (thoughtfully): *"Mom, do you think going to New York is the right decision at the time"?*

HAZEL (placing a reassuring hand on Rachel's shoulder): *"Sometimes, a change is exactly what we need. And who knows, we might find the clarity we are seeking by widening our network".*

The day after tomorrow was looming large as the day of departure. The journey ahead promised a whirlwind of experiences, far away from the shadows that clouded them back home.

The next day unfolded early at Hazel's household, and it was marked with the hustle and bustle of packing and making preparations for the flight to NYC, keeping Rachel and Hazel on their toes for the most part of the day. They found themselves drained of all energy by the time dusk set in. The anticipation of the upcoming conference, coupled with the grueling mental exercise involved in researching and preparing for their paper on the topic of discussion at the conference had left them exhausted. 'The Role of Media and Academia in Spreading Awareness about the Need for Sustainable Development that Doesn't Disturb the Ecology and Culture' was the topic of the seminar and it struck a chord within their hearts.

The sun dipped below the horizon, casting a warm glow over the room as mother and daughter made the final arrangements for the journey. The duo now felt hungry but had no energy left to cook, so they decided to order in. The prospect of a ready-made warm, comforting meal seemed tantalizing and would act like a like a breather from the intensity of the day. But as they ordered pizzas for home delivery, little did they realize, the night had more in store for them than simply pizzas.

Almost half an hour later a knock on the door, signaled the arrival of pizza. Rachel opened the door, eager to receive the pizza delivery but an unexpected visitor standing just behind the delivery boy came as a surprise. A man in his mid-fifties, fairly tall, with a square, spectacled face that bore lines of hardship and struggle stood in the doorway. His eyes held an authoritative gaze... stern, unyielding, not giving away any emotion.

The Pizza delivery boy walked away after handing over the pizza-box to Rachel but the other stranger outside showed no intention of leaving. In fact, he moved closer towards Rachel and held out a card. It seemed to be his identification card and it bore the insignia of IA. The print on the card declared him as William, Senior Field Officer.

WILLIAM (showing his ID): "Senior Field Officer, William from IA".

Rachel and Hazel, taken aback by the sudden intrusion, looked at each other in bewilderment.

RACHEL (curious): " *What brings you here*"?

WILLIAM (with authoritative gaze): "*Good evening Rachel, Hazel. I apologize for the unannounced visit, but I need to talk to you about something urgent. I'm here to disclose about an ongoing plot to sabotage Richard, your dad Rachel, and I need your active involvement to save him*".

HAZEL (wide-eyed): " Oh, Richard is my husband. How did you find out"?

WILLIAM (interrupting her): "*I'm from Intelligence Agency, and it's my job to know about such things. I need your cooperation in matters that should matter you. We must work together to save Richard*".

RACHEL(intrigued and concerned): *"What plot? Who would want to harm dad"?*

WILLIAM (straightforward): *"There's an ongoing plot to finish off Richard. There are unseen enemies at play, and Richard is in danger. Together we can save him. I need your cooperation to save him".*

HAZEL (concerned): *" Oh! What can we do"?*

WILLIAM (leaning in): *"You're attending a conference in New York, correct?*

That's where the final phase of this sinister plot is to take place. So we must ready ourselves.

I'll be on the same flight to NYC as you. We need to work together to expose the culprits and save Richard".

As William disclosed the impending danger, he warned Hazel And Rachel about Udai's true intentions and urged them to be careful and watchful.

WILLIAM (grave): *"Udai is not what he seems. Be careful and watchful. The enemy is closer than you think".*

The revelation sent shivers down Rachel and Hazel's spines, and they were left grappling with a new layer of complexity in their already tumultuous lives.

RACHEL (resolute): *"Mr. William, we'll do whatever it takes to protect Dad".*

William, satisfied by the reply, nodded and left abruptly, bidding bye bye. The mother and daughter, their tiredness momentarily forgotten, found themselves thrust into a situation that transcended ordinary lives. The pizza, now a mere afterthought, lay forgotten as they grappled with the magnitude of the situation that had unexpectedly unfolded in their living room.

The journey to New York City, initially anticipated as a break from their troubles, now bore the weight of a covert mission to save Richard from a looming threat. At least, the present circumstances pointed towards this, if William's words were to be trusted. But even William's intentions and identity, both were questionable. He could be an imposter and there was no way Rachel and Hazel could find out the truth.

CHAPTER SEVENTEEN
READING GOD'S MIND

By now, Hazel and Rachel had realized the hard truth... trust was a rare commodity; and that they could not trust anyone but their own instincts. The next day, around midnight, they set out for the IGI airport to board their NYC-bound flight, scheduled for departure at 3.20 am. Udai and Mihir were with them in the cab to the airport. The city, nicely resting and quiet was draped in fog that affected the visibility.

The quietude and solemnity of the late-night hour was broken only by the soft hum of the car engine. It was a one and half hour journey to the air-port so Udai took upon himself the onus of making the journey delightful with his amusing anecdotes and casual light-hearted banters.

UDAI (with a chuckle): *"You won't believe what happened on my last trip. The airline lost my baggage, and I had to attend a business meeting in borrowed clothes. Quite an experience!"*

No matter how hard Hazel and Rachel tried to maintain a sense of doubt and mistrust towards Udai, the opposite seemed to occur. His simple ways and gentle demeanor, combined with his constant flow of engaging conversation, made it difficult for suspicion and doubts to take root. Rachel and Hazel, despite their resolve to stay guarded, found themselves drawn to Udai's infectious charm. The sincerity in his eyes and the unassuming nature of his tales worked like a subtle enchantment. Udai's humorous tales lingered on, and the journey to the airport seemed to pass in a blink.

As their car approached Terminal-3 of the airport, a dazzling spectacle unfolded before them. The night suddenly turned alive with bright lights, neon signs, and luminous digital billboards glowing all across the lush green landscaped area of the airport. The road leading to the terminal was flanked by beautiful seasonal blooms and manicured greens. Sparkling water cascades with synchronized dancing lights, and decorative water fountains splurging gracefully added to the serene charm. It was a delightful sight to behold, really soothing to the soul. Rachel and Hazel momentarily captivated by the ambiance, forgot their worries. The stress and apprehension that had clung to them seemed to dissipate.

Once inside the bustling terminal building, Rachel and Hazel moved with purpose, their eyes scanning every corner in search of Senior Field Officer William. He was to board the same flight as theirs. Right from the check-in counter, all the way through the security check area, immigration counter, the retail and food court, they remained vigilant, their senses heightened. Their anticipation kept growing with each passing moment. Every face in the crowd seemed to hold the potential of being William.

As they approached the departure pier area, their excitement surged as they finally sighted William. There standing beside the copper sculpture of the Sun God, was William, strategically positioned to catch the attention of people who mattered. Hazel and Rachel, catching sight of him, exchanged a glance filled with relief and determination. His presence exuded a quiet confidence, as if he were a guardian of secrets, ready to lead them through the labyrinth of their quest. Their eyes met with William's, and in that silent exchange, he acknowledged the duo's arrival with a nod, his stern demeanor softening momentarily.

As the boarding announcements for their flight echoed through the terminal, passengers who were spread across the length and breadth of the departure pier, rushed to form a queue in front of the departure boarding gate, and so did Hazel, Rachel, Udai, Mihir, and William. The journey to save Richard from the unseen threats had commenced. The Sun idol, a symbol of radiant energy, stood witness to their resolve.

Midair, Rachel and Hazel struggled to keep an eye on William and Udai. But, the relentless pace of the past two days took a toll. The hum and whir of the engines created a soothing backdrop, like a lullaby, cradling them. The exhaustion they harboured finally caught up with them, plunging them into a realm of deep sleep.

The fatigue-induced sleep stretched beyond what they could have anticipated, and they were oblivious to the marching time. Their reverie got abruptly interrupted by a gentle pat on the shoulder and the cheerful voice of the air steward announcing the final serving of refreshments. Trying to blink away the remnants of their deep sleep, fighting the urge to sleep a little longer, Rachel and Hazel found themselves somewhat disoriented as they responded to the pat that nudged them towards wakefulness. The air steward with a warm smile offered them trays laden with sustenance.

AIR STEWARD (with a smile): "Good morning, ladies. Hope you are doing fine! You both have been sleeping for a long time. Here's a little something to perk you up."

Rachel and Hazel, still groggy from their extended nap, looked into the cheerfully smiling face of the stewardess. The aroma of coffee and the promise of a nourishing meal jolted them awake. Now feeling famished, they eagerly accepted the trays, their gratitude evident.

As they helped themselves to the goodies, Rachel noticed the curious gaze of children across the aisle, fixed on them. They seemed amused by the way their weird sleepy fellow passengers dug greedily into the food served. They stared at Rachel and Hazel with curiosity, occasionally exchanging grins as if privy to a delightful secret.

RACHEL (chuckling): *"We must look quite a sight, Mom, sleeping like hibernating bears and then waking up only to gorge on the food! Kiddos can't help laughing at our sight."*

HAZEL (smiling): *"Well, I'm glad we finally got some rest. Let the kids have their amusement."*

The refreshment quickly done, midair journey continued, suspended between sleep and wakefulness.

Hazel and Rachel tried their best to keep the sleep at bay but soon succumbed again to the seductive balminess of slumber. They slept for hours at length, in what seemed like a drug induced sleep. It was not until the un ebbing cacophony of passengers chattering excitedly, irritated their eardrums, that they finally awoke, but only too confused, as if in delirium. The aircraft was making its descent towards the city of New York, the children in the cabin being the source of gleeful commotion.

The children were apparently on their first flight to NYC and were thrilled beyond words to see the spectacular view from the window as the morning sun bathed the skyline and the sprawling city below in its golden hue. Their animated wide eyed faces were pressed against the window, their exclamations a chorus of wonder. New York City was awakening to a new day, revealing it's enchanting beauty, and the children were enraptured by the spectacle. The golden sunlight accentuated the architectural marvels, casting elongated shadows that danced across the city scape. As the flight descended further, the iconic landmarks, the intricate grid of streets, and the vastness of Central Park unfolded like a living tapestry.

However, for Rachel and Hazel, the transition from the tranquil cocoon of sleep to the lively spectacle outside felt forced. Hazel rubbed her eyes, attempting to shake off the remnants of the sleep that clung to her and blinked in an effort to adjust to the sudden burst of activity around them. Gradually the disorientation gave way and the reality of their arrival in the city sank. Rachel and Hazel embraced the vibrant energy of the moment.

Rachel, at that moment, noticed a glossy magazine resting on her lap. Assuming it a routine in-flight informational and tourist advisory magazine, she cast a cursory glance, flipping through the pages. However, the intriguing article on the very second page titled, "READING THE GOD'S MIND," piqued her interest, prompting her to delve deeper into its contents. The article seemingly urged the reader to embark on a journey of self-discovery by regularly paying visits to churches, the god's abode. The narrative suggested that God's mind is that of the greatest mathematician and implied that the universe with all it's celestial phenomenon are designed to follow mathematical equations of God, the Supreme mathematician. It emphasized the fact that... we humans were but His very special creation meant for spirituality. The article, basically, offered a gentle reminder to the city dwellers about the importance of pausing, reflecting and reconnecting with their spiritual roots.

As she scanned the following pages, she found that it was full of descriptions of the beautiful sacred churches in the heart of the city. Pictures and articles about the various churches of NYC adorned the pages, but what left Rachel flabbergasted were uncanny occurrences of names- Hazel, Richard, Udai, and William as writers or contributors on different pages. Suspicion crept into Rachel's mind. It was obvious, this seemingly innocuous magazine held a clandestine message meant specifically for her.

The articles, ostensibly about churches, appeared to conceal a deeper layer of meaning. Rachel became acutely aware that these names were not accidental inclusions but were deliberately placed and held key to unlocking secrets. Intrigued, Rachel decides to read it word by word and between the sentences. The words held deeper meaning that eluded her at this moment.

The last page of the magazine carried the picture of a particular church and highly recommended all tourists to visit this church. It stated that this church with it's timeless beauty offered great respite from the relentless demands of daily life and provided sacred space for introspection, prayer and communion with the divine. Attending the Sunday mass here must be on the to do list of the visitors to the Big Apple, the writer went on to advise. Rachel, with her sharp analytical skill, taking cue from the article, could deduce that this advice held special importance for her, and that attending Sunday Mass in this church must be on their top priority too. The article bore the name Udai, as the writer, with a mailing address printed alongside for feedback.

Carefully securing the magazine in her handbag, Rachel made a silent vow to unravel all the secret messages hidden in its pages. She understood the need for reading and re-reading, dwelling upon every word and phrase to unearth the deeper truths that lay beneath the surface. The aircraft was about to touch the ground and Rachel was eager to get to the privacy of the hotel room as soon as possible, to do the study and needful research.

As the flight gracefully landed at JFK airport, Rachel and Hazel smoothly transitioned into the Airport transfer service taxi, meticulously arranged by Mihir in advance. The city's energy enveloped them as they embarked on the forty- minute ride, traversing the bustling streets of NYC. When they reached their hotel affiliated with the convention…Westwin Times Square Hotel, in the heart of Manhattan, they felt relieved.

Mihir's thoughtful preparations ensured a seamless check-in process for Rachel, Hazel, and Udai. They settled into their respective rooms, each one a haven with huge windows revealing a dynamic panorama that captured the essence of NYC; sleek, modern skyscrapers itched into the sky framing it with shining glass and steel facades. The bustling streets seen below, alive and pulsating with the energy of Times Square. The Hudson River was visible in the distance, shimmering under the sunlight, a serene contrast to the urban bustle.

As Hazel and Rachel unpacked their belongings, the weight of the transatlantic journey gradually pressed heavily upon them. Feeling the weariness seep into their bones, they both took turns to get under the shower for a refreshing bath. The warm water cascading from the showerheads was a balm to their travel-worn bodies, washing away the fatigue and rejuvenating their spirits. Dressed in comfortable attire and already feeling renewed, they get into the bed to straighten their spine.

However, with a sense of intrigue burning within her, Rachel soon got out of the bed and reached for her handbag, retrieving the magazine she had discovered during the flight. She revealed its weird content to her mom and handed it to her. She watched as her mother's eyes scan the pages and then widening in a mix of surprise and confusion.

Before they could further delve deeper into it, a knock resounded at the door, interrupting their contemplations. A look of surprise crossed their faces as Udai's familiar cheerful voice reached them through the door, his jovial demeanor evident even before they welcomed him in. With a smile on his face, Udai stepped into the room.

"Thought I'd check on you two," Udai exclaimed, his eyes twinkling with enthusiasm. "How are we feeling after the long haul?"

Before they could respond, he launched into a spirited briefing, outlining his plans for exploring Times Square and the evening ahead. The excitement in his voice was palpable as he detailed the itinerary for the next ten days... the list had city tours, convention activities, and the myriad experiences awaiting them in the Big Apple.

As Udai animatedly outlined his plans, Rachel and Hazel couldn't shake off a lingering sense of unease, doubt tugging at their heart. The appearance of Udai at most crucial moments raised suspicions, casting doubts over his intentions. It was as if he had a knack for intruding into their private moments. They pondered at the motives that lurked beneath his jovial exterior. The timing of his appearances seemed too precise, too orchestrated to be random occurrences. They wished they could read his mind! Udai, sensing their unease, left quickly, asking them to come to the dining area after two hours.

In the room bathed in afternoon sun, Rachel and Hazel found themselves once again alone and resumed their scrutiny of the magazine. Their attention drawn to yet another article in it authored by a certain Richard. This article delved into the tantalizing philosophy that every human has a doppelganger…a mirror image, a replica existing in the same realm here on Earth, or in the parallel universes. The article was supported by eerie images of such individuals, who though unrelated, bore uncanny resemblances.

The article went on to point at unique existentialism of each of them irrespective of being mirror images. The notion that each person despite their physical resemblance to one another, possess a unique essence and personality, seemed to be stressed upon, again and after.

This reiteration seemed to hold out a subtle message which Rachel's logical mind inferred to be indicative of look-alikes and duplicates being possibly involved in covert hideous games being played out. The article appeared to be signaling them to be wary of dangers of mistaken identities involving look-alikes.

As Rachel and Hazel grappled with the implications of the article and attempted to decipher the hidden messages in the words of the next page, once again a familiar knock resounded on the door. Udai's restless energy seemed to permeate the air, his frequent interruptions becoming a source of mounting tension. Concealing the magazine beneath a pillow, Rachel opened the door with a sense of apprehension. To her astonishment, it was not Udai but William who stood on the threshold. His demeanor was urgent, and gaze piercing.

He swiftly entered the room, closing the door behind him quickly.

"Do not be alarmed,"

William began, his voice tinged with a gravity that demanded attention.

"Richard is going to check in tomorrow, here in this hotel,"

William disclosed. The implications of his words hanging in the air like a charged electric current. *"He is participating in a conference on data mining at Javits, a part of an ongoing assignment that has him in the role play of a data scientist and researcher, going by the name of Victor."*

The room seemed to spin as Hazel and Rachel absorbed the magnitude of the revelation. Their emotions oscillated between exhilaration and concern. However, William's revelations did not end there. He presented each of them with a handbag.

"Preparation is the key,"

William began, his voice laced with gravitas as he revealed the contents of the handbag… a self-defense kit consisting of pepper spray can, claw nails, Russian knife set and a torch-like stun gun. Each of these items reminded Hazel and Rachel of the dangers that lurked in the corner.

"Ladies, the time has come that you must be alert every second and be ready for the unpredictable. You have to be on your guard and be ready for combat if situations demand it. Armed with this safety kit, not only will you remain safe but you can also avert attempts of assault on Victor, which is not ruled out."

William's voice was firm and commanding as he beckoned them to pick up the stun gun.

As Rachel and Hazel picked up the stun guns, the feel of the cold metal seemed to forebode the perils they faced. William quickly gave them instructions on operating it and then left the room abruptly in a haste, very much like his entry; as if to avert being detected.

As the door clicked shut behind William, the room seemed to close in on Rachel and Hazel, the weight of his revelations setting like a dense fog. A palpable tension now filled the room. Hazel appeared dazed, trying to comprehend the situation while Rachel's fingers grazed the contents of the safety kit, lingering on the cold, hard surface of the stun gun. The reality of their situation was sinking in, and Hazel knew that they stood on the precipice of a journey fraught with uncertainty.

Hazel, typically the epitome of composure, felt a tumultuous whirlwind of thoughts racing through her mind. The revelation that her Richard was going to check into the hotel tomorrow sent ripples of confusion and excitement coursing through her. After twenty long years, her dear Richard would be here near her in flesh and blood, but he was in danger, and she must do everything in her power to safeguard him. She looked at her daughter, and in the exchanged glances, a silent understanding passed between them. Their world had shifted, and the familiar comforts of their everyday lives seemed a world away.

Rachel picked up the stun gun.

"We need to be prepared,"

She said, her voice tinged with a resolute determination.

Hazel nodded, her gaze meeting Rachel.

"We'll handle this together,"

She replied, her voice steady despite the turmoil raging within. Hazel and Rachel found strength in their unity. The road ahead was uncertain, and the shadows of danger loomed large.

CHAPTER EIGHTEEN
THE PURSUIT OF THE ELUSIVE

The dawn's early light streamed through the window, casting a soft glow on Rachel and Hazel as they sat with the magazine and numerous scattered notes spread out before them across the bed. They had spent the whole night pouring over the articles it's each and every word and phrase meticulously dissected in desperate search for clues. Rachel and Hazel's exhaustion was now palpable, dark circles appearing under their eyes, but the urgency of the mission left no room for rest. They must get ready for attending the conference. The Javits Convention Centre beckoned them, so they hastily dressed up after a warm shower.

Just as they were about to step into the shuttle that would take them to the convention center, a familiar face caught their eyes... Richard, their own Richard... he was stepping into another shuttle beside theirs, his arm wrapped around the two gorgeous women who resembled the ones in the photograph back in Delhi. The way Richard held those women, their intimacy was unmistakable. The sight of Richard along with these women deeply hurt Hazel. It was a cruel reminder of the distance that had grown between herself and Richard. Emotions of sorrow associated with estrangement churned within Hazel. The pain was itched on her face, her eyes clouding with heartbreak and longing.

However, the very next instant, as luck would have it, Richard turned and his eyes met Hazel. Their eyes locked and time seemed to stand still for Hazel as a spark of recognition flickered in Richard's eyes. For a fleeting moment, the barriers of time and circumstance seemed to dissolve, and were replaced by the intense emotions that surged between the two. To Hazel the moment seemed like eternity.

But as quickly the spark had appeared in Richard's eyes, it vanished soon too, getting replaced by a look of dismissal as he averted his gaze, boarding the shuttle without a second glance. It struck Hazel like a dagger to the heart. With frail hope shattered, Hazel stood frozen, her heart pounding heavily in her chest. The brief encounter had opened old wounds, leaving her exposed and vulnerable.

Rachel sensing her mother's distress, reached out, placing a comforting hand on Hazel's arm. As the shuttle carrying Richard pulled away, Hazel and Rachel grappled with complexities of love, loss, and the relentless pursuit of the truth. However, without much ado, taking their seat in the shuttle, they too proceeded for the Javits, trying their best to appear composed. They must focus on the conference and, remain vigil at all the times, William's words of caution resounding in their minds.

When they reached the convention centre, they were but struck by the grandeur of it. The expansive foyer was abuzz with activity, as attendees milled about. The bustling crowds served as a distraction from the turmoil within the hearts of mom and daughter. Mihir, the ever-gracious host, who was awaiting them, greeted them with a warm smile and with practiced stride, led them towards the conference room.

As they neared the entrance of the conference hall, murmuring of voices could be heard, punctuated by the occasional burst of laughter and buzz of animated discussion. The atmosphere in the hall was electric, a tangible sense of excitement permeating the air as the participants from various backgrounds converged to partake in the knowledge exchange. Once inside the conference hall, Rachel and Hazel engaged in conversation, exchanging pleasantries and insights with fellow attendees. However, amidst the sea of faces, there was a palpable absence. Udai was conspicuously missing. Hazel scanned the auditorium, hoping to catch a glimpse of him and Richard as well, who seemed elusive too.

The Raging Vortex

The conference was about to begin and all eyes were focused towards the stage, except Hazel's and Rachel's. Their eyes darted around the hall, searching for any sign of Udai, Richard, or William. The esteemed speakers had begun making their entrance on the stage, the hall reverberating with the sounds of claps and thunderous applause. Amidst this crescendo of anticipation and buzz, Rachel's keen eyes caught a sudden, unexpected movement towards the rear left side of the auditorium.

A figure, attempting to conceal itself amidst the shadows, was hastily making its way towards the exit. The abruptness of the departure and the furtive manner in which it moved aroused suspicion. Rachel subtly nudged Hazel, directing her attention towards that figure at the back of the hall. The figure seemed familiar, and soon they realized it was no one else but William...a fleeting flash from someone's mobile phone revealing his face. A shared understanding passed Rachel and Hazel, and with determined resolve, they made the decision to follow him.

Rachel and Hazel rose from their seats, leaving the auditorium through the same door as William. The corridor was dimly lit and as such William was momentarily obscured from view. Hazel and Rachel quickened their pace, their footsteps echoing softly in the corridor. As they neared the exit, they saw William pausing and looking in their direction. He appeared devoid of surprise by their sudden appearance, his gaze steady and unreadable.

As they stood face to face with William, a palpable tension hung in the air, unspoken questions weighed heavily upon them. William beaconed them to follow him, and the trio ventured into the desolate passages of the convention center, away from the prying eyes and murmurs of the conference. The air crackled with a sense of urgency as they walked.

In the shadowy corridors, William disclosed...Victor (their Richard) was in this particular conference room close to where they were standing now. He then led them towards the door of the conference room, and as they peeped in through the upper transparent glass portion of the door, they could see Victor (their

Richard) delivering his talk from the podium. The seminar on data mining was going on.

William took Rachel and Hazel back to the shadowy corridors and apprised them quickly that Victor would leave the conference room in two hours from now and they would have to secretly follow Victor, keeping an eagle's eyes on him as they had to avert any impending attack threatening to silence him forever, William added with nonchalance. Even as Rachel and Hazel processed the gravity of William's words, he beaconed Hazel to come near, and then he motioned for her handbag, his fingers deftly slipping something inside the handbag before returning it to her. The remarkable shift in weight did not go un-noticed by Hazel and she discreetly checked the contents, her fingers grazed against the cold steel of the loaded pistol. William's piercing gaze held Hazel as she looked at him with bewilderment.

Seeing apprehension flicker in Hazel's eyes, William took a step closer, lowered his voice to a hushed yet commanding tone..."*I understand this is overwhelming, but you must keep it,*" William asserted, his voice carrying the weight of experience. "*The enemies we face are powerful and unscrupulous. It's a tool for your protection, and you'll need to be vigilant. The stakes are high, and the path ahead is fraught with danger.*"

As the gravity of the situation settled upon Hazel and Rachel like a heavy shroud, the shadows of the corridor seemed to close in around them. The clandestine mission, in which they found themselves entangled was really a matter of life and death. Rachel, sensing Hazel's unease, placed a reassuring hand on her mother's shoulder, her eyes reflecting the same apprehension.

Rachel took a deep breath and meeting William's gaze, she asked, her voice tinged with a newfound determination, "*What do we do now?*"

"*We stay vigilant,*" William replied, his eyes scanning the corridor as if expecting danger to emerge from the shadows any moment.

William glanced at his watch. "We should return to the convention hall," William advised, his voice low yet firm. "Our absence may already have been noted, and we can't afford to arouse suspicion. The last thing we need is to draw attention to ourselves. Exactly two hours from now Victor will conclude his talk and leave the center and accordingly we will have to time our exit from the conference hall."

Following William's calculated plan, Rachel and Hazel discreetly made their way back to their seats in the auditorium. They seamlessly integrated themselves into the fabric of the conference and waited until the opportune moment presented itself. The atmosphere was charged with anticipation, the seconds stretching into minutes as they mentally prepared themselves for the challenges that lay ahead. As the minutes ticked by, the atmosphere grew palpable with tension.

Finally, the anticipated moment arrived. Rachel, Hazel, and William exchanged fleeting glances, each acknowledging the gravity of the moment and with practiced nonchalance, they rose from their seats one by one, their movements deliberately staggered to avoid drawing attention. They discreetly exit the auditorium and make their way to the main exit gate of Javits center where Victor would pass through any moment now.

In a bid to conceal their identities, Hazel and Rachel hastily drape scarves, pulled taut from forehead to chin. They insured that their features got obscured, rendering them virtually unrecognizable to any onlooker. To complete their disguise, they donned oversized goggles, its dark lenses concealing their eyes and adding an additional layer of mystique to their appearance. William looked at them with admiration. The goggles, with their sleek black frames, lent them an enigmatic air, transforming their familiar faces into inscrutable masks that betrayed no hint to their true identities.

Soon Victor could be seen coming towards the main exit gate of Javits flanked by the two striking gorgeous women who had accompanied him earlier. As Victor walked past them, the atmosphere got charged with a blend of tension and anticipation. Hazel tightened her grip on her handbag, steeling herself for what was about to unfold. Rachel stood poised, her eyes scanning the surroundings for any signs of potential threat.

Victor, along with the two women got into the shuttle bound for the Westwin Hotel, the designated lodging for the attendees of the conference at Javits. Rachel, Hazel and William followed after them, maintaining a discreet distance, and boarded the shuttle from the rear-side door. Hazel and Rachel took seats, a few rows behind Victor's. They felt a surge of apprehension mingled with a newfound sense of empowerment…the disguise, however rudimentary, afforded them a semblance of security, a fleeting advantage in the game fraught with peril and uncertainty. Their eyes concealed behind the tinted lenses, exuded a quiet confidence, their posture betrayed none of the anxiety that churned within.

As the shuttle navigated through the streets of Manhattan, Hazel and Rachel maintained a constant vigil from their seats, discreetly observing Victor and his companions from behind the veil of their disguise. To their relief, Victor was engrossed in conversation with his companions, unaware of the covert pursuers. Hazel and Rachel couldn't help but notice, so very obvious as it was, Victor seemed immersed in the new world of his own with his new partner…it was a world filled with laughter and endearing whispers. The unmistakable chemistry of a couple deeply in love was very much evident.

Hazel's heart constricted at the sight of Victor and his companion. The radiant smile that lit Victor's face, the tender manner in which he wrapped his arms around his companion… each gesture was a dagger to Hazel's already fragile heart. The woman seated beside Victor seemed to bask in his attention, her laughter ringing in Hazel's ears like a cruel taunt.

Hazel's gaze remained fixated on the scene before her, each moment amplifying the tumultuous storm of emotions raging within her. Jealousy, sharp and piercing, gnawed at her as she watched Victor reveling in the company of these women...their laughter seemed to mock her.

Anger simmered beneath Hazel's cool veneer, its flames fanned by the realization of Victor's perceived betrayal. The love they once shared now seemed like a distant memory, overshadowed by the palpable connection he had with his new companion.

Jealousy, anger, and hatred engulfed Hazel, their collective weight pressed down on her chest with suffocating intensity. The man she had once loved, the man who had been her pillar of strength and source of comfort, was now a stranger. Hazel was caught in vortex of conflicting emotions.

In the moment of despair, Hazel contemplated the unimaginable... a desire to end the world tainted by betrayal and heartache. She had the gun, the power to bring an end to the torment and the tormentor with a pull at the trigger. Her grip tightened around the handbag, the leather yielding beneath the pressure as she grappled with the overwhelming urge to confront Victor. The weight of the pistol, a stark reminder of the choices that lay before her.

Yet, amidst the whirlwind of emotions threatening to drown her, Hazel's gaze drifted to Rachel, her daughter, her anchor amidst the storm. The raw vulnerability that reflected in Rachel's eyes mirrored her own, a silent testament to the shared pain and uncertainty that bound them together. Drawing a deep breath, Hazel slowly released her grip on the handbag. Her maternal instincts overshadowed the troubled emotions that sought to consume her. She vowed to herself, she would face the past, confront the deepest fears, and emerge stronger for the challenges that loomed ahead. She shouldn't succumb to darkness, not when Rachel depended on her strength and resilience. The path ahead was fraught with danger and uncertainty, so she had to be Rachel's rock support.

CHAPTER NINETEEN
THE NIGHT OF TEMPEST

As the shuttle meandered through the streets of New York, Rachel's attention remained riveted on Victor and his companions. The scarf that had initially obscured Rachel's ears, was now draped loosely, allowing her to catch every nuance of their conversation amidst the hum of the shuttle's engine. With a keen eye and an attentive ear, she tried to absorb every word, every note of laughter that emanated from the row ahead.

In a stealthy move, Rachel discreetly extracted her phone, positioned it inconspicuously, it's lens pointed in the direction of Victor and the two women and activated the recording, capturing the scene unfolding before her. Her phone documented every gesture, every fleeting expression that crossed Victor's face. These recordings, on future scrutiny, might hold the key to unraveling the minutest nuances, which might be missing, their eyes veiled with emotion and prejudice.

As the shuttle continued the journey, Rachel noticed that the two poised and enthusiastic women companions of Victor, dominated the conversation, their voices rising and falling in a cadence of shared laughter and lively discourse. Strangely enough, Victor's contributions to the conversation were sporadic, his voice mere whispers that eluded Rachel's attentive ears. Each time he spoke, his words were swallowed by the ambient noise of the shuttle. The muscles around Victor's eyes and mouth engaged in a delicate dance, twitching and contorting in a manner that suggested mirth, but his laughter was a feeble decibel that failed to resonate.

Rachel's mind raced, grappling with an unsettling realization. This man who was seated a few rows ahead, although bore an uncanny resemblance to the father she knew, but at the same time aroused a storm of doubt and suspicion within her. Her memories of her dad, primarily constructed from photographs in the family album and hazy recollections from her early childhood, did not match with this man. The familiarity she anticipated remained elusive, leaving her grappling with the disconcerting question... was this truly her father, or a mere semblance.

The physical resemblance was indeed undeniable, the contours of his face, the way he carried himself, and the subtle mannerisms were reminiscent of the Richard she remembered but the essence of Richard, her dad who once filled their home with lively resounding laughter seemed distant and obscured. Her dad used to be a man brimming with vitality, his laughter used to echo with the joyous song of carefree Sundays. Richard's voice, rich and resonant, would envelop Rachel in a comforting embrace. His songs weaved tales of dreamland, prince and princesses that lingered long after the notes had faded.

But the Richard before her now seemed devoid of such vibrancy. His voice, once a melodic symphony that echoed with warmth and affection, was now only muted whispers that failed to rise above the hum of the engine. The laughter that once resonated with unbridled enthusiasm was conspicuously absent, replaced by a stifling silence that seemed to defy the essence of who Richard was. People do evolve and change with the passage of time, but this transformation defied her understanding, and seemed more of an assumed facade with a purpose, which was an enigma. This paradox only fueled her determination to uncover the truth.

Rachel cast a look at her mom beside her. The scarf that veiled her mother's face did little to conceal the furrow of her brows. Hazel's tension was palpable, her posture taut with apprehension. The shared silence between mother and daughter spoke volumes, a silent lament for the Richard they had known. They were bound by the common mission of safeguarding Richard from any lurking threats. They were sentinels, entrusted with protecting a man whose identity seemed to blur with every passing moment.

As the shuttle came to a halt at its destination, Richard disembarked with the two women companions, casting a fleeting glance in their direction. Hazel and Rachel momentarily forgetting that they were indistinguishable, yearned for the tender affectionate look in his eyes. But insignificant, as they appeared due to their veiled faces, they couldn't hold Richard's attention and he moved ahead, consumed in his own world. For Hazel and Rachel, the absence of recognition was both a relief and a pang of sorrow, a poignant reminder of the gulf that separated them.

The shuttle finally pulled up to the entrance of the Westwin Hotel. Hazel steeled herself for the challenges that lay ahead. The afternoon and the evening was set for confrontation that promised to test the limits of her courage and resolve. After alighting from the shuttle, Rachel and Hazel trail Richard to the hotel's lobby, maintaining a discreet distance, their senses high on alert. They watch over as Richard enters the lift, glassy and transparent, the doors closing behind him with a soft hiss. With utmost haste Rachel and Hazel get into the adjacent lift which was glassy transparent too, their fingers poised above the buttons that would carry them to the same floor as Richard. And as fate would have it, Richard's destination turned out to be the same floor that housed their own room! The elevator came to a stop, its doors sliding open to reveal the corridor and their room. Rachel and Hazel watch intently as Richard disappeared from view behind the door of his room, adjacent to theirs.

In that fleeting moment, Hazel and Rachel exchange a glance laden with unspoken questions, their hearts pounding in unison. The shadows of the night that loomed ahead promised to be a night of tempest...the night that would test the boundaries of love and betrayal. Hazel steeled herself for the challenges that lay ahead. The stakes had never been higher, but Hazel was ready to face whatever awaited her. As they settled into their rooms, the air was tinged with apprehension and possibility. The single wall that separated them from Richard in the adjacent room seemed to whisper with the echoes yet to be revealed. Victor was an enigma, his true intentions veiled behind a facade of normalcy and routine.

However, the moment would soon arrive that would unveil the secrets that had long been buried in shadows.

Rachel, sensing Hazel's growing unease, offered a reassuring squeeze of her hand, her eyes conveying a silent message of solidarity and shared resolve... to uncover the truth, protect Richard, and confront the shadows of their past. Rachel knew they were closer than ever to uncovering the truth, a truth that could either shatter their perception or set them free. Rachel's mind raced with questions. Was the man they were following truly Richard, or a mere doppelganger caught in the web of double game? The air was thick with unspoken tension, heightened by the awareness of Richard's presence in the adjacent room. The subtle creaking of the floorboards and the muted hum of air conditioning seemed magnified, each sound getting to their nerves.

Just then the abrupt ring of Rachel's phone pierced the silence, causing them to jump. Glancing at the screen, Rachel's eyes shone in recognition... Mihir's name displayed on the screen.

Taking a deep breath, steadying herself, Rachel answered the call, her voice betraying a hint of apprehension,

"Hello?"

"Rachel, it's Mihir," came the urgent voice from the other end, tinged with evident concern.

"*Is everything alright? I had been searching for you and Hazel... you both were nowhere to be seen in the conference hall. I was worried.*"

Rachel exchanged a brief glance with Hazel, her mind racing to formulate a credible explanation. "Mihir," she began, her voice tinged with a feigned weariness, "*we are back at the Westwin. Both Mom and myself have been having migraines ever since morning. We just needed some rest desperately.*"

There was a brief pause on the other end, as Mihir absorbed the information, and then came his replies. "Alright, if you need anything, let me know immediately. Should I come down over?"

The Raging Vortex

"*Don't worry about us. You continue with the conference,*" Rachel reassured.

"*And Udai? Is he with you? I haven't been able to trace him either,*" Mihir enquired hesitantly.

Rachel exchanged a puzzled glance with Hazel before responding, "*No, Mihir, we have no idea where Udai is. He wasn't with us.*"

"*Alright, just take care of yourselves. Try to rest and recover. The conference is for days, and we'll fill you in later,*" replied Mihir.

Rachel thanked Mihir and ended the call, placing the phone on the table. The soft click of the disconnecting call resonated in the room.

The room was briefly cloaked in a contemplative hush, but then followed a series of sounds from the adjacent room that pricked Rachel's senses. The distinct sound of the rhythmic opening and closing of the door, accompanied by a measured cadence of footsteps echoing down the corridor signaled that Richard and his companions had ventured out into the hallway.

A sense of urgency gripped Rachel and she exchanged a swift glance with Hazel.

"*We need to go out and check what's going on... maybe we'll have to go after them, Mom,*"

Rachel whispered, her voice a mix of apprehension and resolve.

Rachel moved swiftly, retrieving the scarf and goggles used earlier for camouflage. Hazel follows suit, her movement quick yet precise.

Peeking through the keyhole to ensure the coast was clear, Rachel softly opened the door, the muted click barely audible. They stepped into the dimly lit corridor, their senses heightened, every fiber of their being attuned to the task at hand.

As they cautiously advanced, peering around the corner, they caught a fleeting glimpse of Richard, his profile illuminated by the soft glow of the hallway lights. He seemed relaxed, engrossed in conversation with his lady companions unaware of the two figures watching him from a distance. The faint silhouette of another figure ahead, heading towards Richard from the opposite direction caught their attention. The familiar posture, the subtle swagger..., it was undoubtedly Hugo, the Indian fugitive Business man. He was facing charges of financial crimes back in the country, but still had somehow managed to evade extradition by the Indian government. Undeterred, Hugo unabashedly continued to make headlines for all the bad reasons. Hugo shook hands with Richard, embraced him in warm camaraderie, exchanged pleasantries with the ladies and, together the four of them got into the elevator…heading for the parking lot.

Hazel and Rachel swiftly approach the hotel's help desk. With a few rapid exchanges of words with the person at the help desk, they secure a cab and set off in pursuit of the white Lamborghini, which had just started to pull away with Richard in the backseat, accompanied by Hugo and the other two women. The cab trailed the white Lamborghini. Through crowded avenues and streets, the pursuit continued, the two vehicles dancing a delicate ballet through the city's sprawling maze. Finally, after what seemed like an hour-long detour, the Lamborghini began to slow down, its brake lights illuminating with a soft glow in the evening. Rachel and Hazel held their breath as the car came to a halt in front of the Freeland Hotel on 23rd Lexington Avenue. Richard and his companions stepped out, the cool evening breeze playing with their hair as they walked up to the hotel's entrance door.

Maintaining a safe distance, Rachel and Hazel quickly alighted from their cab and rushed towards the hotel entrance. They discreetly followed Richard and his group as they made their way across the hotel lobby to enter Bar Casacalico, nestled on the hotel's second floor. Peering through the ornate railings, Rachel and Hazel watched in stunned silence as Richard and his companions settled into a corner booth, their faces bearing mischievous expression, and they excitedly engage in boisterous exchanges that filled the air. The atmosphere was electric as

The Raging Vortex

patrons mingled, sparkling glasses of wine clinked, and their voices got drowned in the cacophony of sound and lively strain of music.

As the evening wore on, the mood in the bar grew increasingly festive. Richard, his inhibitions seemingly forgotten, joined his companions on the dance floor. He was dancing with fervor, his movements graceful and confident, his hands roaming freely, tracing bodies of his provocative dance partners. The night was still young and the revelry had just begun. The women danced in sync with him seductively, their hands caressing his arms, their lips brushing his cheek. They were reveling in their world of hedonistic pleasure and unbridled passion.

As Hazel observed the scene unfolding on the dance floor, hate coursed through her veins. Richard's sheer audacity of flirtatious acts and the sight of him engaging in an unabashed orgy cut through her heart like a knife. The man she had once admired and loved had become an unrecognizable stranger indulging in a debauchery. A sense of regret gnawed at Hazel's weary soul. In her mind she questioned every decision that had led her to this moment...obviously she had made bad choices, dragging her into the orbit of a man capable of such callousness. She repented marrying this man, having ever met him in the first place. Hazel found herself wishing for a different past, a life without the burden of this man who had caused her so much pain.

In the depths of her despair, a dark thought took root in Rachel's mind. She absolutely wished for Richard's doom, wanting to see him suffer the way she had suffered. The intensity of her emotions overwhelmed her reasoning, and the pain that she felt manifested as a desire to end the source of anguish. In the midst of the deafening music and swirling bodies on the dance floor, she decided she no longer needed Richard. Her hand grappled around the cold metal of the pistol in her Handbag. This was the night of tempest, the night of revenge.

It was a moment of turbulence and madness, and she felt engulfed in a raging Vortex. Hazel, totally blinded by fury, gripped the pistol, finger curling around to pull the trigger, however an abrupt pat on her back startled her to pause midway. Hazel turned around and, was face to face with William, his steady gaze unsettling her for a moment. His presence was unexpected but then strangely enough, it somehow also seemed comforting. Without uttering a word, William signaled Hazel and Rachel to follow him, guiding them out from the chaotic atmosphere of the Night club and into the cool night.

A short distance away from the hotel, William led them to a parked car, its engine idling softly. The urgency of the situation but palpable, Hazel and Rachel quickly get into the back seat. Once they were inside the car and the doors locked, William took to the wheel and drove away from the tumultuous night. In the confines of the moving vehicle, William confided, his voice somber and tinged with gravity,

"I have a big news for you and it comes from credible sources. Richard has defected, becoming a double agent. He's been trading secretive classified information for a life of luxury and decadence. He is a traitor who has betrayed his own country and is liable to be tested before the court of justice. H e certainly deserves to be behind the bars and punished severely."

William's words echoed in the confined space of the car, as it sped through the night. Hazel and Rachel listened in stunned silence, trying to comprehend the magnitude of William's revelation. So, it was now very much an open secret that Richard had indeed been leading a double life, betraying his country... a fact that was consolidated by the events unfolding during the past eight hours. Upon hearing about Richard's defection from William, Hazel and Rachel also immediately recalled the letter containing the disappearing message that had initially alerted them of Richard's defection. The scene tonight in the Night- club was proof of Richard's downfall.

"Our mission has changed,"

William continued, his eyes locked onto theirs in earnest. "We are no longer here to protect Richard. Our goal now is to gather evidence, to prove his guilt and ensure he faces the consequences of his actions."

As the car sped through the night, William outlined their new mission parameters. They were to keep a close watch on Richard, gathering as much evidence as possible without arousing suspicion. William's voice was tinged with regret as he declared,

"As much as it pains us to see Richard in this light, we must prioritize the mission and ensure that he faces the consequences of his actions. Remember, our allegiance is to truth and justice, not to Richard. Our loyalty lies with our country and its security. We need to act swiftly and discreetly. In case Richard suspects and poses a threat, remember you have your pistol, you must be ready to defend or attack."

The gravity of William's words hung in the air, each syllable amplifying the fact the man they had once trusted implicitly had now become their target. The rules had changed, and the stakes were higher than ever. Hazel's fingers grazed the pistol's grip, its cold unyielding presence a reminder of the choices that lay ahead. The line between trust and duty, right and wrong blurred as she grappled with the harsh reality of her situation. The shadow of Richard's betrayal loomed large over her. The path forward was shroud in darkness and it seemed like a daunting journey into the unknown, but now there was no going back at any cost.

The car pulled up in front of the Westwin hotel, William turned around to face Hazel and Rachel in the back seat. His demeanor was a mix of concern and determination. "Alright, ladies," he said, his voice calm yet commanding, "this is where we part ways for now. Get some well-deserved rest; tomorrow will be another challenging day. I'm heading back to the Free World Hotel to keep an eye on Richard. I suspect he'll be continuing his revelry the whole night with Hugo and the ladies."

Once inside their hotel room, Rachel and Hazel changed into their nightclothes and settled in the bed, but the events of the day weighed heavily on their minds, keeping sleep at bay. Hazel stared blankly at the ceiling, the pain of betrayal from Richard was almost unbearable, a relentless ache that refused to subside.

On the other side of the bed, Rachel lay gazing at the time-piece on the wall, her forehead strained in deep thought. She replayed the evening's events in her mind. You may call it intuition or a gut feeling, but she was not convinced that the man on the dancefloor was her father. The aura that her dad used to have was amiss. It was as if someone was impersonating her dad, meticulously copying his walk, the other actions and gestures to replicate him. A nagging question troubled her mind, making her heart race. Was this doppelganger part of a larger conspiracy to ruin her father?

As the night deepened, the room was filled with palpable tension, two souls grappling with a reality they couldn't yet comprehend. Rachel sat up on the edge of the bed, her mind racing as she tried to piece together the intricate puzzle that seemed to be engulfing her family. Each event, each interaction over the past few days played out in her mind's eye. The mysterious letter with its vanishing message had been the first in the domino to fall, setting off a chain of perplexing events. Then there was Udai, suddenly appearing at crucial moments, and now his sudden disappearance only added another layer of complexity to the unfolding drama. And William, with his timely interventions and cryptic advice, seemed to be playing a game of his own.

Unable to sleep, Rachel was drawn towards the magazine. The magazine, with its seemingly innocuous articles, surely appeared to be a coded narrative of their lives. Hidden messages and subtle hints were scattered throughout its pages, almost as if someone was guiding them, nudging them towards a revelation. Her father's new avatar was the final piece of the puzzle, a disturbing confirmation that they were ensnared in a dangerous game orchestrated by forces unknown.

A particular line from the magazine echoed in her mind, the one that urged readers to seek enlightenment in the halls of the churches. Could it be implying that the answer they sought truly lies within those sacred walls?

Determined, she turned to her mother, her eyes filled with a mixture of resolve and concern. Rachel poured out her thoughts,

"Mom, I think we've been played. The man we saw tonight was not Dad. We need to find the truth and I believe the church might have them." Hazel looked into her daughter's eyes, and seeing the determination that burned within, she nodded slowly in affirmation.

"Alright," she whispered, *"we'll go together."*

Hope, even though it was delicate, frail and light as a feather, gave Hazel a courage of conviction. She whispered a prayer, hoping Rachel's instincts were right and that the Richard they knew and love was still within reach, untainted by treachery.

CHAPTER TWENTY
PUPPETS OF MACHIAVELLIAN CHAMAELEON

William, soon after dropping off Hazel and Rachel at the Westwin, headed his car straight for the Free World hotel. As William walked towards the room where his accomplice Benedict awaited him, his footsteps echoed in the hotel's silent hallway.

He gently entered the room with probing eyes and he caught sight of the man who was already there. He couldn't help but admire this handsome man, Benedict; the Victor's look alike. Benedict had removed the make- up off his face, revealing the youthful face of the twenty-seven year old young man. William was, once again struck by Benedict's handsome face with chiseled features that appeared all the more mysterious due to the play of shadow and dim light.

Benedict, the look-alike of Richard had tonight flawlessly assumed the role of Victor. Right now, he was resting in the hotel room, seated behind the vintage desk, meticulously reviewing the series of photographs from the night's event. The room, dimly lit was filled with the faint aroma of aged wood and wine.

Today's performance of Benedict in the double game had been perfect; every gesture, every inflection, Richard's mirror image. Actually, this very uncanny resemblance of Benedict with Richard had set the stage for this game of elaborate deception in the first place.

To William's delight, the plan had been unfurling just as desired. Hazel, in her emotional turmoil, had been completely deceived, unable to discern the difference between her husband Richard and his look-alike. To her, the man she had seen entering and leaving the Javits Centre in the shuttle, and later at the dance floor, were her erstwhile beloved husband, Richard.

"Hey Benedict, great job buddy, the plan is working perfectly,"

William began, his voice tinged with a cold satisfaction.

"Hazel is completely deceived. She has no idea that the man she saw at the Javits and, then on the dance floor isn't her beloved Richard but you, Benedict. She is incensed, convinced that Richard has betrayed her."

Benedict nodded, his expression cold calculated and remarked.

"So good for us, everything is going as planned. Our boss will be pleased."

The anonymous boss, a shadowy figure known to have vast power, influence and ruthless tactics, had orchestrated this elaborate plan using William and Benedict as pawns The Boss aimed to tarnish Victor's reputation irreparably. His malevolent plan to sow seeds of doubt and discord within the Richard's family by planting Benedict, a Richard's lookalike trained to act like Victor/Richard was giving the desired results. The next phase of his plan aimed at pushing Hazel to the brink, making her loathe Richard to the point where she herself would be the instrument of his doom…his demise.

For William and Benedict, it was time to update their mysterious boss, the powerful figure stationed in New Delhi, about the development of the day. Their boss remained veiled in secrecy, and not a soul dared question his authority. William pulled out his phone, preparing to send an encrypted message to their boss, the unseen puppeteer. The message was concise, detailing the evening's events and confirmed that their mission was progressing as planned.

As William hit the send button, Benedict poured them a drink, a silent acknowledgement of work well done. Everything was going according to the plan orchestrated by their enigmatic boss. A satisfied smile crossed William's face.

"What next?"

Benedict questioned, with a hint of unease in his voice.

"Keep Hazel's emotions stirred up."

William advised his tone cold and calculating.

"We need to ensure that she remains convinced of her husband's betrayal. The more chaotic their family becomes, the easier it will be for us to carry out our ultimate objective."

Benedict acknowledged William's instruction with a curt nod. Benedict leaned back in his chair, contemplating the next move. They had come this far, but there was still a lot of work to be done.

The web of deception that were woven was intricate, but they were only puppets operating on the unseen strings of the puppet master, and their loyalty lay solely with the one who pulled the strings. William and Benedict continued to play their roles, dancing with the strings pulled by the Machiavellian master puppeteer. While Richard remained completely unaware of the sinister plot around him; but for how much longer?

In the heart of Manhattan, at this late hour of night well past three, Udai sat hunched over a secure communication device in a dimly lit room. Udai was a seasoned operative with deep ties to the IA headquarters in Delhi, and had been Richard's trusted ally in the past.

More than four years had passed since Udai and Richard had exchanged any word with each other, busy as they were working on disparate assignments. However, only two months back, Udai got assigned with the delicate task of safeguarding Richard's family in wake of a sinister plot of enemies to end Richard, the greatest asset of IA, along with his family.

Well, Udai was now on official calling to secure the safety of these above-mentioned three individuals who were running great risk to their lives. As such, he was decrypting a highly classified message he had just received from IA headquarters.

The walls of the room where he sat were covered with soundproofing material to muffle any sound and keep it from escaping out from the room, creating an intense secure atmosphere.

Udai's mind raced as he grasped the message. The message was a directive for him to go ahead with the next stage of the plan. According to the Plan Udai had to act swiftly to convene a clandestine meeting with three very important people Richard, Hazel and Rachel.

The time had come when Udai must shed the cloak of secrecy and reveal his true-identity before Hazel and Rachel, initiating the next course of action.

First thing first, Udai sets upon to put the plan into action by quickly sending a cryptic message to Richard, instructing him to come over to the prayer hall of the local church of Manhattan by 7 am sharp, the day after tomorrow, it being Sunday.

The enemies, still under veils of secrecy, aimed to topple the pillars of the country's security, therefore Richard along-with his family were one of its prime targets. In wake of all this, Udai had taken upon himself the onus of not only safeguarding Rachel and Hazel but also preparing them for the imminent challenges that loomed ahead, uniting them together in a concerted effort to counteract the machinations of their shadowy adversaries.

With each passing moment of the restless night, Udai felt the weight of uncertainty growing heavier. There was no time to be lost. He made a swift decision to pay an unannounced visit to Rachel and Hazel's room the first thing in the morning and apprise them about his true-identity; also about the perilous situation that they were in. After all, their cooperation was essential for the plan to succeed.

Earlier during the day, Udai had witnessed the dirty game that the enemies played out at Javits center to manipulate Hazel and Rachel using the lookalike of Richard. While the real Richard was busy with the ongoing conference in one of the halls of Javits his look alike was masquerading outside the hall, deceiving Hazel and

Rachel into believing that their Richard was now a fallen man of low character, leading a hedonistic life of excesses.

The unfolding events at the Javits center today had only confirmed Udai's worst fears about the enemy tactics, and now he deemed it crucial to reveal everything about the impending threats to Richard and his family.

Determined not to leave anything to chance, Udai orchestrated in his mind the whole sequence of the meeting that was to take place in the church, day after tomorrow on Sunday. Udai had laid the groundwork for the meeting meticulously, choosing the church as the meeting point because of its perceived safety and sanctity. The meeting in the sacred confines of church would be the first step towards uniting the family against the forces that sought to destroy them.

Then, during the meeting that was to ensue with the trio Richard, Hazel and Rachel in the church, Udai was required to share with them the next course of action according to the plan. Success of the plan as well as its execution depended on their concerted actions with proper coordination. In the world of covert operations, even the best-laid plans could fail with slightest mistake.

Udai had, on earlier occasion too attempted alerting Hazel and Rachel about the enemies' dirty game by stealthily placing a specially curated magazine with hidden markers and messages on Rachel's lap while she was asleep in the flight to NYC. However, he was not sure she had been able to comprehend it. Anyway, during the ensuing meeting on Sunday, Udai was going to tell Hazel, Rachel, and Richard everything about the double game.

Udai's pulse quickened as he glanced once more at his phone; the encrypted message to Richard was still marked as "unread," though an hour had passed by. The execution of the plan, the meeting, and everything hinged on Richard's acknowledgement, a confirmation that remained conspicuously absent. As the night wore on, Udai knew that time was running out. Every moment counted, and the need for immediate action was palpable.

The successful meeting in the church on Sunday was the first step towards uniting the family against the forces that sought to destroy them. The safety of Richard and his family hinged on this meeting. Udai silently prayed that Richard saw his message and the plan worked so that Richard's family emerge unscathed from this intricate game of espionage and treachery.

God was indeed merciful and quickly answered Udai's prayers... the notification just received on his phone confirmed that Richard had read his message. An 'OK' sign message from Richard flashed on the phone. The plan was set in motion. Udai was greatly relieved and braced for restful sleep.

Obviously, it was not only Udai who was still awake till this hour of late night, but Richard was awake too busy as he was making preparations for leaving early this morning for Roosevelt island to attend the lunch at Marc's holiday home. However, now upon seeing Udai's cryptic message on the phone that asked him to come to the local church day after tomorrow for an urgent meeting slotted to commence by seven am, Richard's mind set racing... various permutations and combinations of questions and doubts crisscrossed in his head.

Interestingly, besides Udai and Richard, this late night hour in NYC also saw William and Benedict awake, preparing for the next phase of their boss's plan, their minds focused and their hearts cold. The task that lay ahead for them was dark and dangerous, but neither of them dared to question the boss's orders. They were puppets and their loyalty to their Machiavellian elusive boss was absolute.

However, time would soon unfold to reveal the fact that they were all living in a world where loyalties were fleeting and trust was but a luxury!

CHAPTER TWENTY- ONE
UNVEILING SECRETS IN HOLIDAY HOME

The city of dreams, NYC was gradually stirring to the vibrancy of a Saturday morning, seductive with it's unique weekend charm. The streets below were abuzz with the energy of early risers, spirited joggers and leisurely strollers, all headed for Central Park. Sidewalks too brimmed with locals and tourists alike, seeking the perfect cup of coffee or exploring the array of shops. The day finally dawned when Victor, Clara, and Sandra were to embark on a journey to Roosevelt Island. They were readying themselves for attending the luncheon at Marc's holiday home. Their attire, carefully chosen, embodied grace and sophistication, befitting their roles in this high-stakes charade. Victor had instructed Sandra to play the role of his wife, while Clara would portray his daughter.

As they left Manhattan, the atmosphere in the car was a mix of anticipation and curiosity. They couldn't help but wonder why a billionaire like Marc would have a holiday home on Roosevelt Island, a place not typically associated with holiday retreat location feel. It seemed an unusual choice given the island's history.

The car wound its way through the bustling streets of Manhattan, headed straight for Roosevelt Island. It was an hour drive through the best part of New York City. They passed by Central Park, the Metropolitan Museum of Art, and Bethesda Terrace, before making it to the outskirts of Queens, then eventually crossed the Brooklyn bridge over the river East to finally approach Roosevelt Island. The closer they got, the more the island's enigmatic allure tugged at their senses.

During the journey Clara and Sandra researched the island's history, uncovering tales of its past. Roosevelt island was known as

Blackwell Island back in 1839, notably having housed the New York Lunatic Asylum during the mid- nineteenth century. By 1890 this island was home to prison, a charity hospital, men and women almshouses, a workhouse, a smallpox hospital, a chapel, and the second largest insane asylum in the country.

Though, the island had in present time transformed into a bustling location with modern residential buildings surrounded by beautiful landscaped sprawling lush greens but still it was a stark contrast to holiday retreat locations like California and Florida.

When Victor, Clara and Sandra arrived at Marc's holiday home they were met by a picturesque scene; a luxurious apartment condominium nestled in a tranquil corner of Roosevelt Island. The façade displayed opulence, but the island's reputation cast a shadow over the idyllic setting.

As Victor, Clara and Sandra stepped out of the car, they were greeted by Marc's manager, a man of impeccable manners, well-versed in the art of receiving guests. He showed them around the lush, meticulously landscaped grounds of the sprawling condominium with the grand imposing main building of splendid architecture. Moreover, it seamlessly blended with nature's beauty, a testament to Marc's refined taste.

The journey from Manhattan had given the ladies time to prepare and gather their thoughts. Clara and Sandra, adept in their art with practice over the years carried themselves with poise, ready to play their roles to perfection. As they strolled across the estate, their attire and demeanor emanated grace and sophistication that impressed the manager. It was a subtle act they were required to put up as they were players in a world where appearances must conceal greater truth. They were experts in their art with practice over the years and as such carried themselves with poise, ready to play their roles to perfection.

The manager led them into the luxurious penthouse, leisurely taking them around, show casing its grandeur, from the sprawling living area adorned with exquisite art pieces to the magnificent library filled with rare books. They all couldn't help but admire the intricate detailing of the penthouse. The choice of art and décor was impeccable, reflecting Marc's exquisite taste as an art collector.

As they entered the elegant dining room they were met with the sight of Marc, his wife Athira, and their son Mihir all impeccably dressed, exuding an air of refinement.

MARC (Extending a hand to Victor): *"Welcome once again, Victor. I trust the journey was comfortable?"*

VICTOR (Shaking Marc's hand): *"Absolutely, Marc. Your apartment is truly magnificent."*

The host and the guests exchanged pleasantries and the atmosphere was convivial. The guests were led to the dining table and the luncheon commenced with polite conversation, each member engaging in it. They spoke of the island, the weather and the journey that had brought them here.

As the meal progressed, their discussion turned to more esoteric matters. Marc, known for his passion for the art, delved into the world of music and fine art, sharing anecdotes of his encounters with renowned artists and musicians.

However, it was Athira, Marc's sophisticated wife who impressed them the most with her conversations that were truly engaging, touching upon a wide variety of subjects ranging from current affairs, world of politics to avant-garde art, cinema and painting. She was far from being pedantic unlike the majority of elite class wives. Victor was particularly struck by her profuse knowledge of psephology.

Amidst the clinking of cutlery and the soft murmur of conversation, the manager came in to discreetly announce the arrival of yet another guest, Vyom. Marc's family greeted this newcomer with evident pleasure, suggesting that his presence had been eagerly anticipated.

Vyom was introduced as a scholar, historian and spiritual healer...a silver-haired man whose lined face hinted at wisdom and experience. His mystic aura added an intriguing dimension to his presence, making him appear much older than his years.

MARC (Smiling warmly): "Ah, Vyom! So glad you could join us. Allow me to introduce you to our guests, Victor, Clara, and Sandra".

VYOM (Bowing slightly): "It's a pleasure to meet you all. Marc and I go back a long way. We share a passion for history and the mysteries that it holds".

Vyom was seated next to Marc at the dining table and everyone's eyes were riveted at him. He radiated a rare kind of aura that was hard to overlook.

As Victor and Vyom exchanged pleasantries with each other, surprisingly, the two of them were instantly attracted towards each other, struck by an overwhelming feeling of brotherly love, a bonding, an experience that was nothing short of Deja Vu.

In fact, Victor's senses were triggered in a unique manner the moment Vyom had entered the dining hall...his psychic senses detected something unusual about Vyom. Vyom seemed to have an energy that resonated with his own, a connection that transcended the mundane. Vyom certainly possessed gifts and powers similar to him, and if this got confirmed then, in a way Vyom was a one of his own tribe; and this realization set his mind spinning.

To this day Victor had known just one person (besides himself) who had the gift of psychic powers, his grandpa, late Major General Ronald Mathews. Victor was deeply attached to him and couldn't help but feel nostalgic whenever he reminisced about the good old days spent with grandpa.

His grandpa had been a retired army officer, acclaimed for his valor and nobility. Victor vividly remembered the stories that his grandpa used to tell. They were mostly about his daring missions in the army. In 1953, grandpa had served in the Infantry Brigade, under the commandership of great Manekshaw at helm. Their troupe had carried out dangerous missions at the Indo China and Indo Pak border, and emerged victorious. Then again, in 1971, grandpa had taken part in the Indo-Pak war that led to the creation of Bangladesh.

Grandpa was unique as he had immense psychic abilities, which he kept concealed from the outside world, but which he secretly used for the general good of the masses... Clairvoyance, the ability to see beyond the physical realm, and metaphysical ability of psychokinesis. As such, he could influence the physical world with the power of his mind, orchestrating simple acts like moving lightweight objects across the table, or causing a door to slide open or close, all with his power of visualization. Aided with these psychic powers he could perceive the world and the worldly affairs beyond the ordinary. He could sense truths, deceit, dangers, and foresee the future. For good reasons both grandpa and his family kept his powers a guarded secret within the closed doors.

Victor had been the favorite grandchild of his grandpa, perhaps because Victor was the only one who had taken after him by virtue of being born with the psychic abilities (though not as full-fledged but only a small fraction). He was still unique like his grandpa due to this 'gift' inherited in genes.

However, these psychic powers set him apart from his classmates from a very early age, making him a loner but at the same time made him bond closely with his grandpa, like no one else. Victor loved and adored his grandpa, memories of him making him nostalgic with the sense of longing.

Surprisingly enough, Vyom's presence was having a certain kind of influence on Victor where he found himself overpowered with a similar deja vu kind of nostalgia, and with an even greater intensity than ever before. However, Victor's face didn't reveal his inner state of mind.

After the slow sumptuous lunch, the diners were led towards the study room. It was a room steeped in knowledge and replete with rare artifacts. The study was bathed in the soft glow of antique lamps, their warm lights casting intricate patterns on the rich wooden furnishings.

In the study, Marc approached a heavy book and handed it to Vyom. Vyom's eyes lit up with curiosity and reverence. The book was a collection of handwritten parchment papers bound together. It bore angular writings, strange otherworldly symbols and unsettling illustrations. The book, Marc remarked, was laden with ancient knowledge and secrets awaiting to be unlocked.

MARC (With a hint of excitement): "Vyom , my friend, this book is a treasure I stumbled upon during my recent travels. I believe it holds the key to something extraordinary".

VYOM (Examining the book with a scholar's eye): "You are always lucky to get hidden gems, Marc. Let's see what this one reveals".

As Vyom and Marc delved into the ancient tome, Victor's discerning eyes examined the whole study. He caught sight of something unusual, a large crystal ball placed on a table nearby. It resembled the mysterious spheres often depicted in movies as tools for predicting the future or peering into the past. Victor's curiosity had been piqued, and he found himself drawn to the shimmering sphere on the table, wondering what secrets it might hold.

Marc, the observing host, perceived Victor looking with curiosity, his gaze fixed upon the crystal ball. Marc understood that this was an opportunity, a chance to introduce Victor to the enigmatic world of the crystal ball gazing.

MARC (Smirking): *"Ah, Victor, so this crystal ball seems to bewitch you. It's a little relic Vyom brought from India".*

With a gracious smile, Marc then extended an offer to Victor.

MARC (Eyeing Victor's intrigue): *"Victor, my friend, have you tried crystal ball gazing? It's a journey into the mysteries of life. If you haven't then I suggest, you should try it now at least once".*

Victor, always eager to experience and learn new things, considered the offer. He recognized that this was not merely an exercise but an opportunity to take a deeper peek into the secrets that surrounded Marc and his associates. He nodded in agreement, ready to venture into the uncharted territory of crystal ball gazing.

Marc turned to face Vyom and gestured him to start the crystal ball gazing session. Vyom, the scholar, the historian, and a psychic too (according to Marc, with claims of him possessing power for clairvoyance) took charge of the session. With an air of reverence, Vyom began by invoking cosmic energies, his voice a soft murmur of sacred chants that filled the room.

Vyom, the revered member of the group, had an aura of enigma, his eyes pools of infinite wisdom that held secrets that transcended generations. It was believed that he possessed the power to communicate with the supernatural, to bridge the gap between the living and the dead!

Soon the room grew strangely still, and an eerie silence enveloped the gathering. Victor felt a palpable shift in the atmosphere, as if boundaries between reality and supernatural were dissolving. Every one present in the study were silent witnesses to the magical ritual that was in progress.

As the room reverberated with the soft incantations of Vyom, Marc couldn't help but feel more than satisfied. Things were unfolding according to his meticulous plan. This was a pivotal moment. The crystal gazing session that had just begun was actually a test to determine whether Victor was fit for induction into the covert society, Illuminav!

CHAPTER TWENTY TWO
THE CRYSTAL BALL GAZING

It was a customary practice within the secret societies to delve into the past and assess the background of the potential members before extending membership.

Marc had summoned Vyom specifically for this purpose, for he knew Vyom's expertise in crystal ball gazing would reveal the hidden facets of Victor's life.

He had carefully orchestrated this gathering for the crystal ball gazing at his Roosevelt Island estate, a place away from the humdrum of the city, a place of recluse and isolation where the boundaries between reality and the mystical blurred. Vyom was engrossed in invoking the unseen spirits for their cooperation in successfully conducting the crystal ball gazing session.

VYOM (In a hushed tone): *"We seek to peer into the past, to unlock the mysteries that lie hidden within the depths of time. The crystal ball will be our guide, a window to the bygone eras"*.

As Vyom continued his incantations, the crystal ball began to emit a soft, ethereal glow, its surface shimmering with an otherworldly light. It seemed to come alive, and within its translucent depths, wisps of mist swirled and danced, taking form and substance.

The room itself seemed to shimmer, as if veils between worlds were being drawn aside. The study became a chamber of secrets, where the past and present converged in a dance of cosmic energy.

VYOM (Speaking with reverence): *"Let us open the doors to the past, to the mysteries that lie within. Together, we shall journey into the depths of time"*.

As Vyom continued his incantations, the crystal ball now began to vibrate, its surface seeming like a pool of liquid glass. Victor fixed his gaze upon it, feeling a sense of wonder and trepidation.

Clara and Sandra watched with a mixture of awe and doubt, unsure of what they were about to witness.

The room held its collective breath, each person a silent spectator to the magic that was about to unfold.

VYOM (In a hushed tone): *"We call upon the cosmic energies that bind time and space, grant us the vision to gaze into the past. Let us peer into the river of time and witness the moments that have shaped our lives".*

The crystal's magic began, unfolding within its illuminated spherical body, as claimed at the onset the personal moments of the participants. Mihir being the first one to appear in the crystal. The image, like vivid scenes from a movie, revealed him taking a stroll, hand in hand with a Lady. Their affection for each other very evident by the way they held each other's hands tightly in a firm clasp. The very, next moment, they wrapped their arms around each other in a loving embrace, their chest close to each other's, their heart beating in unison. Embarrassment washed over Mihir when the scene went on to show him lip locked in a passionate intimate kiss with the Lady.

Victor, however, was even more embarrassed than Mihir and watched in bewilderment. The Lady engaged in a kiss with Mihir was no one else but, his own Rachel! He was damn sure that she was his Rachel not only because she resembled her mirror image but because he had caught sight of the unique pendant and the chain hugging her slender neck. This was the same chain and pendant set that he had gifted to her, on her birthday. The crystal's revelation had left him dazed.

MIHIR (Blushing): *"This is ridiculous"!*

Well, it was not only Mihir and Victor, but Marc and Athira too seemed taken aback, by the revelation. The crystal ball had unveiled an episode that they were not at all prepared to see.

Athira seemed shocked by the crystal's revelations. And even as she was trying to come to terms with the crystal's revelations about her son's love life, her own image started showing up in the crystal's gaze!

Well, there was her image on the crystal wherein she bore a distressed look. She seemed to be in a jewelry store. She could be seen surrounded by security staff. A burly man in the store had pulled out a chair for her to sit. She looked weak and about to pass out.

Athira watched her own image in the crystal with bewilderment and fear; for her secret was on the verge of being revealed. Actually, she had lost her diamond wedding ring while trying out new rings in that store the day before. The shop had promised to retrieve it within two days after scrutinizing CCTV footage and a thorough search of the premises.

ATHIRA (In her mind): *"Will the crystal reveal the truth about my lost wedding ring? I haven't told Marc yet; maybe this is high time I disclose".*

As she watched with bewilderment, the vision in the crystal changed to give a close-up view of her designer Tarun Tahiliani peach gown that she had worn to the shop that day. The crystal's image focused on the ruffled and ornate sleeve of her beautiful gown and her diamond ring showed entangled within its folds; hidden from plain sight! Athira's eyes widened with realization; it was indeed a Eureka moment. Her ring had always been with her, tangled up in her gown! She couldn't wait to rush to her closet and retrieve the lost ring from the folds of the gown.

As the session of revelations continued, the view in the crystal shifted and it now showed Marc standing in a hotel room, holding an important looking file. Five men along with a woman had gathered around him, all holding a similar looking file that prominently displayed in bold letters, the word "ILLUMINAV" printed on top. Also, the files bore the label, 'PROJECT- Benaulim Art and Cultural Convention Centre'.

These seven people seemed to have assembled there with a mission. They were studying a miniature model of a building, kept in the center of the table. The model was a futuristic building and looked like a grand convention center. Perhaps they were discussing the blueprint of the project, delving into the minuteness, it's architectural details before embarking on it. It was obvious to clever Victor that the project was of constructing a convention center in Benaulim and that Marc was associated with Illuminav, the secret society. What he would later come to know was that this venue of convention centre would provide a perfect cover-up for holding covert meetings of the secret society, ILLUMINAV.

Well, the crystal had in many ways revealed to Victor of Marc's hidden identity and his association with ILLUMINAV, the secret society. It was however not clear whether everyone else present in the study room, could comprehend it.

Victor glanced at Marc, however, surprisingly Marc, appeared unruffled by this revelation and looked deep in the eyes of Victor, a gentle smile on his face. Actually Marc was satisfied that crystal ball had done what words perhaps couldn't have achieved with this amount of clarity and certainty… it had revealed for sure his hidden identity as a member of Illuminav.

MARC (Calmly, spoke to himself): *"Well, it seems the crystal has done enough revelation for today".*

Victor, who had heard of the covert societies, but had never before witnessed anything to prove it, this profound revelation came as an enlightenment with evidence. Now all his doubts were dispelled. The existence of Illuminav was no longer debatable; it was a reality!

The next moment, the scene in the crystal changed and images flashing in the crystal now captured the footage of a gathering at the bustling Jacob K. Javits Convention Centre, a renowned hub for conference and exhibitions in the heart of New York City. The crystal ball provided the bird's eye view of the event of yesterday

The Raging Vortex

with Victor as one of the key speaker. Victor, dressed in sharp professional attire was seen speaking with eloquence about the ever-evolving world of data science. The audience seemed rapt, hanging on to every word he spoke. Victor was in the spotlight, at the heart of this gathering.

The annual conference on Data Science was in progress with Victor, the distinguished data scientist addressing the audience, sharing his insights and expertise in the field of big data, data mining, and predictive analytics. The room was abuzz with discussions, presentations, and knowledge sharing among the attendees.

However, the vision within the crystal ball took an unexpected turn. It surprised Victor with the shift of focus; now flashing the scene just outside of the Javits Centre. It displayed throngs of visitors making a beeline for security check and screening before entering the Centre. Victor's discerning eyes caught two familiar faces in this crowd on the crystal's projection…two captivating women who looked far from ordinary tourists. They were walking side by side with an unknown man, crossing the intersection just outside the Javits Centre at the same time when the conference with Victor at helm was in progress within its folds. These beautiful women were undoubtedly Rachel and Hazel, the women Victor most cherished.

It was an unexpected twist in the vision. The crystal's projection confirmed Rachel and Hazel's presence in the heart of New York City and was almost a riddle, waiting to be solved!

Victor thought to himself,

"They couldn't just be here in NYC as mere tourists or casual observers. Instead, they appear to be there with a purpose, a mission that ran deeper than a simple visit".

As the image continued to play out on the crystal ball, Victor's mind raced with speculation. The two women walked in tandem, seemingly in deep conversation with a mysterious man. The air around them seemed charged with significance, hinting at a secret agenda.

Victor pondered as he watched the scene unfolding in the crystal.

"What could have drawn Rachel and Hazel to New York City? The Big Apple was a place of limitless opportunities and grand events, perhaps it was a television show, or a media event that had drawn Rachel to NYC, and Hazel must have accompanied her for the sake of shared experiences." Thus, Victor surmised with his analytical mind.

But this particular revelation of the crystal ball raised more questions than answers. It was indeed a puzzle, adding another layer of intrigue to an already enigmatic situation. In the world of espionage and hidden agendas, nothing ever was as it seemed, and Victor knew there was more to this story than what met the eye.

However, Marc, the host of the luncheon and crystal session was more than satisfied. The crystal ball's revelation confirmed Victor's claim of being a professor of data-science at a private University of New York State. So, now that Victor's identity lay bare. The purpose of crystal ball gazing had been fulfilled. Marc signaled Vyom to end the session.

Vyom sounded a clap, and with that, the crystal returned to its normal inert self with normalcy claiming the study-room too. Most significant secrets had been laid bare by the crystal, leaving the people present in the room grappling with the revelations and the newfound knowledge that bound them together. The city beyond the window of the study gleamed with the promise of another lively New York evening, but inside the heart of the luxurious penthouse, intrigue and mystery reigned.

With a sense of purpose. Marc initiated the conversation.

MARC: *"Gentlemen and ladies, I must say it has been a great pleasure to have you in my humble abode and I hope you all have enjoyed this session with Vyom.*

I've always been fascinated by the intertwining of art, mysticism, and intellect. Today's gathering has been a beautiful amalgamation of all of

The Raging Vortex

these. I'm sure all of my esteemed guests must have enjoyed the delicious dive into the world of gastronomical delights arranged by my lovely wife, Athira. She is my most beautiful, intelligent, loyal companion, my rock support, and the greatest love of my life."

As Mark's monologue and conversations continued in the study room, each person present in the room secretly pondered upon the revelations of the crystal ball. It had cast its light on their own lives or the lives of the other people who mattered, revealing more than what they all had bargained for. Victor, for that matter, was more perturbed than others present in the room. His thoughts wandering around Rachel, Hazel and the unknown stranger with them. Things were not quite in place and pointed towards impending trouble.

Marc was quick to notice the change in Victor's disposition and was curious to find out the reason for it. He also needed to talk to Victor and disclose about the chief motive behind today's meeting. Therefore to attain privacy for discussing the pressing issues, he urged his wife to take the Ladies along and show them around the other floors of the penthouse, especially the art and music room. Ladies seized at the opportunity for diversion and quickly set out with Athira while the men remained in the study room.

Now, Marc turned his attention to Victor. Addressing him directly, Mark broached the topic of the illustrious secret society Illuminav. In a hushed tone, he disclosed his affiliation and extended an invitation to Victor to join their clandestine rank. Vyom too acknowledged his association with Illuminav and extended his card to Marc, urging him to join. The card bore the words in print 'life coach and spiritual healer' below Vyom's name and his phone number was also there.

Mark revealed that the society was embarking on a noble venture; that of constructing cultural cum convention centres at historically significant but neglected places all across India. The first one to come up would be the Ben O'Lim Cultural and Convention Centre at Benaulim, a place steeped in the legendary tales of Parshuram.

Mark passionately delved into the lore of Parshuram at length:

"Legend had it that Parshuram, an avatar of Lord Vishnu, donated all of the land on earth to Maharshi Kashyap. He then persuaded Lord Varuna, the God of Waters, to raise a land mass from the sea exclusively for his devotees and followers, a command which Varuna conceded. The Konkani coast and much of the land of Kerala rose up from the sea for Parshuram. Nevertheless, Parshuram required more land mass and therefore he shot an arrow into the sea, asking the waters to retreat up to the point the arrow was shot. The sea god, Varuna, relented, leading to the creation of Goa. The place where the arrow landed came to be known as the village of Benaulim; Bena in Benaulim comes from the Sanskrit word 'Bana' which means arrow. But, of course, there is much more to the credit of Parshuram and there are more facts about Goa than what pages of history textbooks contain. The envisioned cultural cum convention center would highlight the various aspects of forgotten history. This center in Benaulim would illuminate the glorious past and be a beacon, showcasing the richness of Vedic and Puranic legends associated with this land."

MARK (firmly): *"Victor, our paths have led us to this moment. I propose that you join the illustrious Illuminav Society. Your expertise and influence could significantly contribute to the success of the society's mission of preserving our country's supremacy and cultural legacy".*

As the weight of Mark's words lingered in the room, the air crackled with anticipation. Victor ostensibly contemplated the proposition presented by Mark. Nevertheless Victor knew in his heart that Mark's proposition was in tandem with Victor's goal of infiltrating the group (in this case, it had turned out to be a secret society) and unearthing it's deeper secrets and purpose.

VICTOR (looking contemplative): *"Mark, I think I should value your offer. This is indeed a unique opportunity. Let me consider it further".*

MARK (smiling): *"Victor, give it a second thought. Only few are extended this privilege. It will be an honour to have you among us though".*

VICTOR (with a decisive nod): *"Mark, if you insist so, I accept this offer. Let's embark on this journey together".*

MARK (extending a hand): *"Welcome to Illuminav, Victor".*

As Victor shook Mark's hand, the study room witnessed a pact forged in trust and good faith. The secrets of Illuminav now had another keeper, Victor. But Marc was not aware that Victor was a keeper of far too many secrets.

As the evening progressed, Victor couldn't shake off the feeling of a growing unease and a sense of being overwhelmed with having too many secrets to hold and too many pressing issues to address. The imminent meeting with Udai the next morning dominated his thoughts.

CHAPTER TWENTY-THREE
THE TWIST IN THE DOUBLE GAME

It was a crisp Sunday morning of November. The streets were alive with excitement as the city prepared for the Veteran's Day parade. Victor, clad as a parade participant, inconspicuously strode through the vibrant streets, heading toward the chapel on 29th street. His disguise was a necessary measure to avoid being identified by potential enemies who might be lurking, ready to strike at any given moment.

Meanwhile, Rachel and Hazel, too, set out for the meeting, trending the sidewalks and making their way to the chapel. On any ordinary day, the distance was a mere ten-minute walk, but today the crowded streets on the special occasion of Veterans Day, prolonged it more than usual. Hazel and Rachel, aware of potential threats from adversaries, had taken special precautions, concealing their identities by assuming the visages of parade participants.

As they made their way to meet Richard after twenty long years, a mix of emotions swirled within them. They were grateful to Udai for being the guiding light in the darkness that had been engulfing them and had threatened to swallow them. Yesterday morning, Udai had come to meet them in their hotel room and had made significant revelations before them, laying bare the intricate web of deceit and manipulation…the double game, the existence of Richard's look alike, Udai's connections with the IA and about the righteousness of their Richard, the man himself.

Rachel, who had been suspicious over Udai's intentions, now grappled with a sense of vindication. She regretted having doubted Udai, a true friend who had tried to protect her from the sinister game, but at the same time also felt relief at finally understanding the truth. Nevertheless, she very much felt betrayed by William's involvement in the evil scheme.

Hazel, walking alongside though looked composed on the outside, deep down inside she felt drowned in sea of remorse. She had been too naïve to judge Richard wrongly, to allow doubt to creep into her heart even though Rachel being much younger had maintained unshakeable faith in her father throughout their tumultuous journey. The realization that her suspicions were unfounded brought a sense of guilt. As she approached the chapel, she sought solace in the hope of healing old wounds and forging a new beginning with her sweet Richard.

As the crucial meeting in the chapel loomed on the horizon, Udai's trusted operatives maintained a constant vigil over every move made by Hazel, Rachel, William and Benedict. The intricate plan devised by Udai was unfolding according to his carefully crafted design. The previous day, early in the morning, Udai had assumed the guise of a room attendant and discreetly visited Hazel and Rachel in their hotel room. Quietly, without uttering a word, beaconing them to maintain silence, he had passed on to them a detailed letter that disclosed the presence of a spying device planted in the handbag that needed to be deactivated to allow them to communicate freely without the fear of risking eavesdropping. The letter had gone ahead to disclose Udai's true identity as an DIA agent, and it further shed light on the complex web of deception. It strongly warned Hazel and Rachel about the imperative need to maintain secretive silence until the spy device was deactivated. After going through the letter and comprehending the situation, Hazel had surrendered her handbag to Udai, who quickly traced out the concealed spy device embedded in the stun gun, and with utmost stealth deactivated it. William had been eavesdropping on mother-daughter's conversations and tracking their movement with these devices.

Having regained Rachel's and Hazel's trust, Udai outlined the strategy to entangle William in his own deceitful game. The master plan involved two female operatives, disguised as room attendants, who would come to Hazel and Rachel's room, early on Sunday morning. Assuming the identities of Rachel and Hazel, these operatives would stay behind in the hotel room, while actual mother daughter duo Hazel and Rachel would leave the hotel room guised as room attendants. The female operatives would stay in the room the whole day, feigning illness whereas, Rachel and Hazel would assume the attire of parade participants and proceed for the clandestine meeting with Richard in the chapel.

So, working upon Udai's plan, the following morning, Hazel and Rachel leave the hotel room for the church. The female operatives stay behind in the hotel room and activate the spy device within the stun gun. They play pre-recorded conversations between Rachel and Hazel, creating a convincing illusion of Rachel and Hazel's presence in the room. This was aimed to mislead William (who had been eavesdropping over Rachel and Hazel through the compromised stun gun) into believing that Hazel and Rachel were in the room itself. This way, William was getting ensnared in his own double game.

Richard, who was still on his way to the chapel, blended among the throng of pedestrians. While Udai waited in the church, acting just like any other touristy visitor, engrossed in observing and appreciating the architectural marvel of the chapel's facade. However, his keen eyes meticulously scanned every person entering the chapel's premises, aware that Richard could be one of them cloaked in disguise. His sharp instincts were proven right as he spotted a tall, bearded man approaching the church. Recognizing the familiar signs of Richard's clever disguise he hastened his steps and intercepted the bearded man he believed to be Richard. Using a unique and secret code, a form of sign language reserved for IA operatives, Udai greeted the man.

To his delight, the responses came in the same coded sign language, confirming that he was indeed Richard. In a covert exchange, Udai updated Richard about the intricate double game involving William; shedding light on the events surrounding Hazel and Rachel. Udai conveyed the imminent arrival of Hazel and

Rachel, urging Richard to prepare for the much awaited reunion that was about to unfold.

For Richard, life always seemed to hold out surprises, much like the impending meeting with Rachel and Hazel. As Richard reflected on the unpredictable nature of life, his countenance portrayed a facade of calm and composure, a veneer carefully maintained for the outside world.

Yet, beneath this outward facade, a storm of emotions raged within him. His heart skipped a beat as Udai disclosed the actual arrival of Rachel and Hazel on the scene: information that injected both anticipation and trepidation into his composed demeanor. The prospect of reuniting with his wife and daughter, especially under the current circumstances, stirred a mixture of emotions that were visible only to those who could penetrate the mask of calm exterior.

Richard had never anticipated this sudden twist. He had pictured himself, giving Hazel and Rachel a heartwarming surprise during the festive season, enveloped in the warmth of Christmas cheer at home. However, the hand of fate had dealt a different card, leading him and his family down a path fraught with danger and intrigue. Life, it seemed, had scripted a narrative far more complex than the simple joy of family reunion.

Now, not only was Richard caught up in a complex web of espionage and double game, but his beloved wife and daughter were also ensnared in the dangerous situation, forced to assume roles they hadn't fathomed. The circumstances had taken a sharp turn, and the joy of family reunion was now shadowed in secrecy and espionage. Richard, nevertheless braced himself for the long awaited emotional family reunion and the challenges that awaited him in this unexpected chapter of life.

CHAPTER TWENTY-FOUR
THE PREMONITION

William and Benedict, having successfully executed the initial stages of their boss's intricate plan, found a moment of reprieve at a vibrant dance bar. The fact that Rachel and Hazel were rendered bedridden with flu had eased the tension that had gripped them during the past few days. It temporarily offered them relief from the constant chase, keeping track of every movement of the two women. In the dimly lit ambience of the bar, they reveled in the music and lively atmosphere, letting the strain on their nerves dissipate, at least for a while.

However, on the other hand, disparately enough, their boss Walter, sat alone in his Delhi house, dousing down the strongest blend of spirit in his home's bar. The fiery liquor burned his throat, but the sensation was nothing compared to intense burning in his chest inflamed with seething hatred for Richard ablaze in it. He wanted to destroy Richard, and take his life. But he didn't want Richard's blood on his own hands, either. He had conspired with William to equip Hazel with lethal weapons and to instigate her into shooting down Richard, her own husband out of hatred and retribution. They were waiting for the right fateful moment when Richard would come to meet his dear Hazel, the love of his life, only to be shot dead point blank by her.

Walter brooded over the slow unfolding of his plot in NYC as Rachel and Hazel remained confined in the hotel room. He suspected some hidden intention behind Rachel and Hazel remaining confined on the pretext of being unwell. Walter analysed this new twist with skepticism and contemplated the next moves in his elaborate game of deception.

However, Walter's key accomplice, William unmindful of all this, reveled in NYC along with bar dancers. He indulged in unrestrained drinking and uninhibited dancing as if there were no tomorrow, much to angst of Benedict who was growing weary with the overindulgence in the excess of wine, and the company of too many frivolous women. The shocking revelations that had unfolded few days following his arrival in NYC lingered in his mind, and he grappled with coming to terms with the new chapter that had abruptly opened in his life.

Amidst the ostensible gaiety, Benedict's thoughts meandered around Rachel and Hazel and he felt a surprise upsurge of emotion and concern for them. He had developed a soft spot for them. He felt genuine sorrow for the mother-daughter duo who had endured so much hardship and misery though they deserved the best of life. He felt even more so miserable now, realizing he had unwittingly become an instrument for ushering more troubles into the mother-daughter's already troubled lives. This realization gnawed at his conscience. To him, these women embodied virtues, kindness and warmth; and were deserving of a fate far kinder than the one unravelling before them.

They were most scholarly, beautiful and the nicest individuals he had met in life thus far. Acutely aware of his humble roots, Benedict reflected on his lack of higher education in stark contrast with well-educated good Samaritans, Rachel and Hazel. His own life journey traced back to a tragic past, with him suffering the loss of his parents in a road accident during his fifth-grade year. Henceforth, raised by his uncle and aunt who were trapeze artists in a circus, Benedict was steered towards a life in the circus, mirroring their legacy.

His education was truncated after the twelfth grade, and he had to reluctantly step into his aging uncle's shoes as a trapeze artist. His world was defined by rigorous discipline of circus life, marked by moments of misery, dangers, greed and unrelenting struggle. Despite the challenges, Benedict excelled in his unconventional career. However, a longing for education persisted, compelling him to enroll for a graduate course in an open university. Juggling with his performances in the circus, Benedict pursued a bachelor's degree in physical education, eventually earning the degree. But fate had few more macabre planned and Benedict watched with horror as his aunt succumbed to a fatal fall during a trapeze act. His uncle overcome by grief and, due to the limitations of his own aging body got lured to drugs, which only worsened his condition. One fateful morning he just didn't wake up from his sleep. After his uncle's demise, Benedict severed his ties with the circus, embracing a new chapter in life as a physical education teacher in a school. However, destiny had other plans for him.

It had been little over a year into the new job as teacher with a reputed school in Central Delhi and Benedict was already beginning to get noticed for his excellence and dedication. However, soon fate took a twist. One evening Benedict was engrossed in thoughts of planning for the next day as he was crossing the road while returning home from school when Walter, seated behind the wheels of his car, spotted Benedict at the red signal. Struck by Benedict's uncanny resemblance to Richard, (albeit twenty years younger) Walter was driven to a frenzy of sorts; breaking the signal, he impulsively hit Benedict with his car.

However, after a few moments, as Benedict lay immobile unable to get up and a crowd started to gather around his car, Walter realized his mistake and quickly stepped out of his car, offering apologies. Taking swift action, he carried injured Benedict into his car and rushed Him to a nearby hospital. He generously shouldered all the hospital expenses over his treatment and, also made it a point to drop in daily to cheer up ailing Benedict till he recovered.

Later on, introducing himself as a Movie director with aspirations, Walter extended an intriguing offer to Benedict... a lead role in his upcoming spy-themed movie. However, there was a condition; Benedict was required to quit his current school job and undergo rigorous training for the lead role, which required him to portray an active fifty-year-old spy of great refinement and eminence.

Benedict, unsuspecting and eager for opportunity, accepted the offer, marking the commencement of his exhilarating journey into the world of cinema. Little did he realize that this offer for a role in the movie was actually a trap leading him into an abysmal labyrinth of an intricate web of Walter's machinations where he would be used as a pawn in a malevolent plot against Richard and his family. Walter carefully kept his ulterior motives hidden from Benedict as it risked to alter the trajectory of Benedict's life once again.

As the shooting of the movie began, Benedict found himself alongside co-stars William, Bella and Cassa along with others. Benedict's acting schedule and training for the role and acting under directorship of Walter was rigorous, requiring him to embody the persona of a fifty year old spy with great details. The movie centered round the lives of the spy, his wife and daughter.. He was also required to camouflage himself with lots of makeup applied on his face to look like the fifty-year old spy.

As the shooting progressed, the storyline required them to shoot at different locations offshore in NYC, ranging from Westwin Hotel to Javits Center. But, as fate would have it, Walter suddenly developed chest pain and on doctor's recommendation he had to stay behind in Delhi while the crew left for NYC with one Mr. William as the newly appointed director.

Upon arrival in NYC, Benedict soon becomes acutely aware of the strange fact that shoots were always being done when a particular duo of women were very much around them. Every time he along with Sassa and Bella enacted the scripted roles, whether be it at Westwin, or at Javits, surprisingly enough, unfailingly on each occasion, the same woman duo were very much around. Later on, he came to know the names of this women duo, Hazel and Rachel.

Benedict also accidentally happened to overhear secretive conversations between William and Walter. Moreover, he realised the hushed conversations occurred not only between William and Walter, but also with someone whom William referred to as 'the boss'. Benedict got suspicious and questioned William about 'the boss', to which William nonchalantly opened up, disclosing the fact that 'the boss' was a powerful don based in Delhi and happened to be the mysterious producer of their movie.

Indeed, the glamour of the film industry masked darker truths. The boss, who was based in Delhi dictated terms over Walter and William, forcing changes in the script. Benedict and all co-actors were expected to adhere to these changes and provide progress updates to 'the boss', usually after midnight.

This puppetry orchestrated by the underworld don required them to dance to his tunes. Later Benedict learned from William that shooting for the movie was in fact simply a tool for unleashing the Boss's sinister plot to destroy the spy Richard and his family.

'The boss' was however generously compensating William and the film troupe for their loyalty and services with tempting offers of wealth, wine and women, which William urged Benedict to wisely accept just as he had done. He also pointed out that they had no other choice and could lose their lives if they dare defy the don's directives.

CHAPTER TWENTY-FIVE
THE VANISHING SILHOUETTES

Walter was restless and pacing frantically in his home office. He was vexed, as all his operatives stationed in the Big Apple, including the usually reliable William, had lost track of Richard, Rachel and Hazel. The trio had mysteriously disappeared, leaving no trace behind. The quiet hum of the city outside seemed to mock his frustration as he pondered over the sudden disappearance.

Walter, sensing an impending storm on the horizon, was gripped by a feeling that something big was about to unfold in the game of shadows. The question lingering in his mind kept echoing, "What could it be"? Walter's mind raced through the possibilities. However, instead of succumbing to anxiety and waiting for the events to unfold, Walter the mastermind, decided that it was high time to take matters into his own hands. The situation called for a bold course of action, a countermove, something more significant and shocking.

In the world of espionage and clandestine operations, Walter knew that being one step ahead was not merely an advantage but a necessity; and sometimes offense is the best defense. The time had come to implement the most Machiavellian plan. The game that he had been playing on a small scale with Hazel and Rachel will now be played on Bigger level. The chess board was set and Walter was prepared to make his move that would not only match the impending big event but surpass it in shock and magnitude.

Walter made a swift hand movement on the encrypted communication device before him that connected him to William and initiated a call. A hushed silence engulfed the room, broken only by the faint hum of electronic signals. The call was connected and Walter's steely voice resonated through the encrypted line as he issued his orders to William to act on Plan D without wasting any time.

William nodded grimly as he deciphered Walter's coded message. His eyes gleamed with determination as he got ready to set in motion plan D. The plan involved Benedict impersonating as Victor, plunging head- on into the pulsating heart of New York City's nightlife. He had to immerse himself in wild exploits, hobnobbing with influential figures of immense power. This was aimed to show Victor in low light as a depraved man…, a defector not worthy of trust by anyone…, a cancer or a gangrene that needed to be extracted and destroyed.

In the heart of the city, Benedict, acting on plan D, assumed the role of Victor and entered the opulent world of New York's elite nightlife. He mingled with influential figures, attending lavish gatherings where power and influence intermingled. The objective was to tarnish Victor's image beyond redemption.

As the night progressed, Benedict artfully engaged in wild exploits, ensuring his every move got noticed by socialites and power brokers. His actions were being captured discreetly by camera of William's operatives including William. The capture would paint a vivid portrait of a man succumbing to his vices.

In exclusive clubs and dimly lit corners, Benedict associated with individuals of questionable repute, emphasizing Victor's supposed descent into moral decay. Clandestine acts of disloyalty and defection were being enacted like a dark theatrical production to portray Victor as a malignant force that needed excision.

As the night reached the climax, Benedict's exploits grew more audacious to make headlines that would reverberate far beyond the city. William was satisfied with the manner in which the plan had worked seamlessly and he set off to culminate the act by sending the videos of the masquerade to his master.

Courtesy William, in a matter of seconds and few taps on keys of the laptop, Walter was now equipped with video footage of

Benedict. It was a concoction of scandal, vice, and treachery woven into the tapestry of Victor's false identity.

Walter turned to his laptop and made a few purposeful taps on the keys. At one final tap, fabricated leaks with sensitive pics of Victor aka Benedict, along with other tainted double agents and defectors were spread on the internet, intending to create a sensational narrative of betrayal and espionage.

Walter gloated with delight as he released the incriminating videos across the vast expanse of the web, taking precaution of assuming the cloak of anonymity. He had finally successfully exposed the dark side of Victor to the world. Victor, who was a defector and a double agent working within the intelligence community, a big threat to national security.

By morning, the news headlines would be screaming about the traitor Victor. It would catch the public's attention, and add pressure on the authorities to apprehend the elusive Victor. Walter knew it very well that in today's world controlled by the media, it is easy to destroy anyone by polluting the minds of the public with wrong stories and narratives about the person concerned.

CHAPTER TWENTY-SIX
SLOW DANCE WITH THE ENEMY

As Walter reclined on his bed, a sinister smile crept across his face. The success over implementation of his plan D filled him with a dark sense of satisfaction. The digital realm was overflowing with video footage of a tainted version of Victor that suited Walter's narrative; a distorted image that would cast a perpetual shadow on the man's character.

Gloating with joy, but also feeling exhausted Walter decides to rest. The soft embrace of the sheets welcomed him as he settled in, but sleep was elusive. The moment his head touched the pillow, as usual a floodgate of memories that deeply hurt once again burst open, washing away the sleep.

The haunting memories took him back to those perilous days in the troubled valley, on one of the assignments that had tested the limits of endurance. Victor too was together with him on this assignment, sharing the trenches with him as they tried to hide from the terrorists who were on lookout for them. Perhaps, a failure of intelligence services, which are at times but unavoidable, had led to leaks about their real identity, putting them in life threatening situations. The vivid images of the night engulfed in chaos and gunfire emerged from the memory with painful clarity and danced slowly before the eyes of his mind. It was a slow dance with the enemy. Undoubtedly, bad memories are like enemies that cause hurt, destroy the peace of mind, break the heart, and could even kill.

A shoot out had erupted. The terrorists had unleashed a hail of bullets on unsuspecting civilians, as they sought Waltor and Victor who they assumed were hiding in one of the houses . The duo, Walter and Victor had however evicted the house they had been operating from and taken refuge in the trenches, attempting to shield themselves from the onslaught.

In the midst of the turmoil, as bad luck would have it, a stray bullet found it's mark, piercing Waltor's right leg. He fell to the ground, incapacitated and vulnerable. Desperation etched across his face, he turned to Victor, seeking aid in his dire moment.

However, Victor's response was a chilling betrayal. Ignoring Walter's plea for assistance, Victor callously abandoned him, disappearing into the night. Walter became a captive in the terrorist's camp, enduring months of unspeakable torment. But the wound inflicted by Victor's betrayal cut deeper than any physical wounds, and the scars left by his abandonment festered with each passing day, becoming a relentless hurtful companion.

However, by a stroke of luck, it so happened at the camp one day, a bomb kept in the cache of the terrorists went off by itself. The blast was highly impactful and claimed the Camp, destroying it totally but, somehow Walter was unhurt. Soon army personnel arrived on the scene and discovered Walter. Rescued by an army unit, Walter was transported to a hospital where his physical injuries were treated, but the emotional wounds inflicted by Victor's betrayal remained unhealed.

Walter remembered with detest, the day he had first set eyes on Victor. It was a dark rainy night twenty years ago in Goa. Victor was then Richard, a civil servant, and Walter was Alvin, who alongwith three of his colleagues from 'Intelligence Services' had secretly met Richard and his wife in his quarter to counsel and urge to join Intelligence Services. The day heralded the end of Richard's career in civil services and his entry into the Intelligence Services.

Walter had been instrumental in inducting Richard and furthering up his career graph by guiding him in his initial days with the new role. They had even collaborated over two assignments before this fateful one, and had been trusted allies.

The betrayal by a trusted ally had left an indelible mark, a gaping wound that grew larger and more sinister as time passed. Often during the lonely hours of the night, Walter felt suffocated, engulfed in a raging vortex that threatened to drown him. This was exactly the mental state Walter was at the moment and as the memories kept haunting and tormenting him, Walter reached for a bottle of sleeping pills. The bitter-sweet pills provided a temporary refuge, casting a numbing shadow over the ghosts of his past as he succumbed to the elusive embrace of sleep.

CHAPTER TWENTY SEVEN
ANAHATA, THE UNHURT, THE UNBEATEN

While the city outside was abuzz this Sunday morning, getting ready for the Veteran's Day parade, the morning at Marc's household was full of promises for the start of a great relaxing day. The aroma of the brewing Darjeeling tea and oven-fresh rosemary-basil-thyme focaccia bread delightfully wafted in the house. Marc breathed in deeply, indulging in the pleasant titillation to his olfactory senses.

Marc had just returned home from running his pets, a German shepherd and a Golden retriever around the sprawling campus of the society. Exhausted, he now comfortably slouched into the rattan chair of his balcony and picked up the glass of fresh sparkling goji berry juice that had been waiting for him. Today was the seventh day of the fourteen-day juice therapy that Vyom had put him on and he was already feeling the change…, improved energy, mood and focus. Vyom had recommended this drink to him for protection against all age-related problems and had sworn by its multiple health benefits. Vyom was in many ways, Marc's best friend and confidant besides being his Guru and life coach.

Meanwhile, in the cozy ambiance of their living room, Athira sat down with her son, Mihir, determined to unravel the secrets concealed within his heart. The crystal's revelations, particularly the lip-lock incident aroused many questions in Athira's mind and they were weighing her down.

In the privacy of their home, Athira gently probed, urging Mihir to share the truth about his relationship with this young lady with whom he had shared an intimate moment. Athira made it clear that if he was serious about her, she wanted to know more about the special woman and expressed her desire to meet her.

Mihir, with sincerity in his eyes, chose to lay bare the secrets in his heart. He began by disclosing the details of his ongoing project and collaboration with Rachel, Hazel, and Udai. Athira listened attentively as her son painted a vivid picture of his dream collaborative project and his association with Rachel. He spoke of Rachel with warmth as he revealed the depth of his feelings.

With candor, Mihir confessed his love for Rachel. He expressed his desire to introduce Rachel, along with Hazel and Udai, to their family. Athira, though surprised, recognised the sincerity in her son's words.

Taking a proactive stance, Athira proposed inviting Rachel, along with Hazel and Udai, for high tea in the evening. She wished to waste no time to meet the woman who held a special place in her son's heart and to understand the depth of their connection. Mihir, grateful for his mother's understanding, readily agreed to arrange the meeting.

Excitement reverberated within the house as Athira shared this new revelation with her husband, Marc. The couple discussed the new dynamics and it was unanimously agreed upon to host a high tea in the evening to welcome Mihir's guests into their homes. In a spontaneous decision, Marc also decided to extend an invitation to Vyom and Victor as well. He believed that including Vyom in the gathering would not only be a desirable courteous gesture but it could also be a wonderful opportunity for assessing the vibes and compatibility of Mihir's lady love by making use of Vyom's psychic and intuitive powers.

Well, Marc had a very specific purpose behind inviting Victor. Strategic and forward thinking as he was, he envisioned the gathering, the bringing together of Victor and Vyom, as an opportunity for initiating the collaborative work towards deciphering the book of scriptures.

Eagerly anticipating an evening filled with meaningful associations and shared insights, Marc dialed Victor's number with great enthusiasm. Simultaneously, Mihir tried to reach out to Rachel,

Hazel, and Udai. Unfortunately, leaving aside Vyom, all the other calls remained unanswered or failed to connect, prompting Marc and Mihir to leave sms and voice messages on their respective voicemails, hoping for a prompt response. Marc and Mihir were oblivious of the fact that their invitees, ensnared in double game of the enemy, had assembled secretly in the chapel and were devising a plan to come out of the trap.

Victor, Udai, Rachel and Hazel had put their phones in the silent mode to shield them from the outside world and preserve the sacred ambience of the chapel. It had been little over an hour since they had met and reconnected with each other in the serene confines of the sacred place. Immersed in the profound sense of peace, they were grateful for the unexpected serendipitous reunion in such a divine setting. The pain and remorse of past years had dissipated, leaving behind a surreal sense of blissfulness. After the session of reflection and discussions the group decided to check their phones.

As they unlocked their devices, a symphony of vibrations ensued, causing them to quickly look at their phone screens. Each of them discovered the missed calls and the warm invitation messages from Marc and Mihir, seeking confirmation of their presence. Realizing the synchronous timing of the messages, an intriguing feeling crept in, and out of curiosity they discussed the messages and were surprised to realize that they were all invited to the same address and at the same time. This coincidence added an extra layer of intrigue causing a fresh discussion to ensue. Each one of them shared an insight into the nitty-gritty of their recent work engagements, the related acquaintances, and profile of their respective host. Eventually, connecting the missing pieces together, they came to the conclusion that Marc and Mihir must be related..., perhaps father and son.

About half an hour later, Marc and Mihir received messages from each of their invitees including Vyom, expressing gratitude for the invitation and confirming their enthusiastic presence. Marc and Mihir were delighted to see the messages. The event was scheduled

The Raging Vortex

to commence at five in the evening, providing exactly six hours for the preparations and anticipation to build. Meanwhile, Athira with her characteristic flair, was already deeply engrossed in setting things, readying for the sundowner affair.

Amidst the anticipation, Mihir couldn't contain his excitement and promptly called Rachel to brief her about the real motive of the gathering. Mihir had as yet not disclosed to Rachel about his parent's presence in NYC and about their holiday home in Roosevelt Island. Rachel simply knew that Mihir's parents were based in Gurgaon and were into the pharmaceutical business. She had no inkling of the vast wealth and the elevated status held by Mihir's parents, the owners of Atharva Pharmaceutical Company. As Mihir opened up and shared details about the evening plans and the real purpose behind the meeting, Rachel listened attentively, still unaware of the surprise that awaited her in the upcoming hour.

By half past five in the evening, the sundowner at Marc's home was in full swing. The hosts warmly welcomed their guests, setting the stage for a delightful evening. After initial meet and greet sessions, the group settled down and began deeper conversation, fostering an atmosphere of camaraderie.

As the sun dipped further, live musicians took to the stage. The musical notes emanating from their musical instruments created a harmonious symphony that guided the feet of the group members into a slow and graceful dance. The classical melodies resonated through the air, creating an enchanting ambience.

The host led the guests to a beautifully set buffet table where they all treated themselves to gourmet delicacies, followed by a tea ceremony, adding an elegant touch to the festivities.

After an hour of chit chat over the tea, Vyom, with his air of tranquility surrounding him, took center stage, capturing the attention of an eager audience. His voice deep and resonant, carried the weight of wisdom as he embarked on unraveling the secrets to leading a fulfilling life.

"Life is inherently simple, my friends,"

Vyom began, his eyes reflecting a profound understanding of life.

"Yet, we make it complex by chasing success, wealth, name, and fame. Human intelligence, the god's greatest gift to us, is like a double-edged sword, which, unfortunately though is mostly wielded to divide us... we humans... into class and creed with conflicting interests, instead of forming a peaceful communion directed towards spiritual growth."

As Vyom spoke, a hush fell over the audience, captivated by his words. His insights penetrated the layers of conventional thinking. Vyom then led the group into a transformative session of yoga on the spacious deck of Marc's penthouse. Out on the deck, they were met with a spectacular sight of the evening sky coloured in hues of amber, pink, tangerine and lavender. The setting sun cast a golden glow on them as it continued its descent below the horizon. The air carried a hint of November chill that was refreshing.

Vyom guided the group into the intricacies of meditation, starting with chanting of the sacred sound of Om. "Om," Vyom softly chanted, setting the tone for the meditation. The group closed their eyes, tuning in to the harmonious vibration. The air resonated with the soothing vibrations of "Om" as each member took a series of deep breaths and focused on the rhythmic flow of the sound, allowing it to permeate their entire being.

"Now, let's delve into the realm of Anahata ," Vyom continued, his eyes gleaming with serene intensity. He spoke of the significance of the heart chakra (Anahata) according to yogic philosophy, and it's association with love, compassion, and emotional wellbeing. The term 'Anahata' as such translates to 'unstruck' or 'unhurt' in Sanskrit, and unbeaten in Hindi.. He guided the members to visualize a radiant light at their heart centers (the epicenter of love and compassion), expanding with each breath.

"Feel its warmth radiating with growing intensity, enveloping your entire being," he urged in a guiding tone. "Now, let the sound of Om fill this space with love and compassion," Vyom requested, and the group immersed themselves in chanting, their voices creating a soothing echo. Vyom elaborated on the significance of chanting Om and Yam, the sound associated with the heart chakra, emphasizing it's ability to open the channels of love within oneself and radiate it outward. Its regular practice is known to foster peace and connection with the universe, and enkindling love and compassion.

Only, how wonderful it would have been if the echo of their chanting could reach beyond the immediate space, reverberate across a thousand miles and penetrate the barriers of hatred and deception...to strike a cordial note in Walter's heart.

But these were the times when the world around was shrouded in dichotomy. While here, Marc and his guests were immersed in the serenity of guided meditation, finding solace in the simplicity of the moment...contrastingly, not far away, William and Benedict were enmeshed in a web of duplicity and deception driven by their allegiance to a man whose motives were anything but pure.

Call it destiny or power of incantation...the far reaching effect of chanting Om...Benedict, all of sudden feels an overwhelming surge of courage, conviction and strength... and he finally steels his resolve to break free from the shackles of his sinister boss; and abandon the double game of deception.

Benedict, for a long time, had found himself standing at the crossroads between loyalty and morality, pushed to the brink by the unbearable weight of his conscience. But due to lack of courage had been unable to follow the voice of his conscience. Lacking in boldness to take a stand for himself he remained a puppet in the hands of his malevolent boss. However, suddenly he felt charged, and valour coursed in his veins. He resolves to shun the acts of deception. He finally takes the tough decision to abandon the game of treachery and vows to protect Rachel...to reveal the boss's sinister plot to Rachel; even if it meant risking his own life. Benedict wanted to save Hazel and Rachel but first of all he needed the perfect moment to escape the vigilant eyes of William in order to sneak out from the den.

CHAPTER TWENTY-EIGHT
FORGING NEW ALLIANCE

It was only by the wee hours of the Monday morning that Willliam and Benedict returned to their hotel room, exhausted from the relentless charade of the night. William, in a state of inebriation, leaned heavily on Benedict, who guided him through the hallway to their room. As the door closed behind them, the room became a cocoon of whispered intentions and clandestine plans. William stumbled in his drunken stupor as he tried to sit at the work desk to start the laptop. According to the protocol, he had to contact their boss to report on the progress of Plan D and get further instructions from him.

However, alcohol had taken its toll on William, rendering his finger movements erratic, and he struggled to press the correct keys, but his attempts were futile. With a dismissive gesture he handed over the job to Benedict, giving him the needed instruction and the necessary code to initiate the call to their elusive boss.

Benedict, with a mix of apprehension and determination, took charge of the keyboard, entered the code disclosed by William and initiated the call. The room echoed with the connecting tones. By the time the call connected, William's snores were already resonant in the room... he was in deep slumber, oblivious to the unfolding event.

The call rang persistently, but there was an eerie silence on the other end...no response whatsoever from the person on the receiving side. Benedict initiated a fresh call again but it went unattended too. The suspense hung in the air, creating an atmosphere fraught with uncertainty and tension, as Benedict anxiously awaited any sign of acknowledgement from the boss.

The absence of response only added to the tension, heightening the suspense. Benedict found himself caught in a strange situation with boss remaining unresponsive, and William in strong clutches of sleep oblivious of everything.

As the seconds went slipping by, in that indecisive moment suddenly Benedict realized, the opportunity he had been waiting for had finally arrived. It was the perfect time to sneak out; to abandon the treacherous path he had been coerced into. William was apparently totally stoned and did not pose any threat. The wall clock, a silent witness to the unfolding scene, held its breath as Benedict quietly approached William, skillfully extracted his gun from the holster, stepped out of their shared room, and locked the door behind him.

When Benedict reached Westwin, it was already six in the morning. The light of dawn streamed through the glass panels and casted a golden glow on the corridors as Benedict approached the reception desk The atmosphere in the lobby was hushed, with only a few early risers moving in the expansive space. Approaching the reception desk, Benedict greeted the staff with a composed demeanor belying the turmoil within and requested the person in charge. "Good morning. I need a favor," Benedict began, choosing his words carefully. "Could you please call the occupants of room 1707 and inform them that their friend, William is waiting in the lobby area? There's an urgent matter that needs to be discussed."

The receptionist, well accustomed to handling various requests, nodded professionally. He picked up the phone and promptly dialed the requested room number. Rachel, in her room, received the call and as the receptionist delivered the message, his words echoed.

Rachel, quick-witted and, always on alert, instantly messaged Victor about the unexpected call from William. Victor was quick to read the message. The urgency of the situation rang through the text. Victor got ready, and geared up for reaching Westwin, eager to witness all that might unfold.

While Benedict still stood waiting in the lobby, his thoughts racing as he anticipated the crucial meeting with the ladies that was about to take place. Every passing second felt like an eternity, and nervous tension gripped him as he feared the possibility of being apprehended. Benedict again approached the reception and requested for a pen and paper. With trembling hands, he began to hastily pen down his observations about the game of deception that has been playing around the ladies, detailing each plot intricately, the involvement of boss and William, his coerced participation, and his subsequent escape. The letter was a plea for forgiveness and a sincere expression of desire to help Rachel and Hazel.

Benedict nervously waited, and almost fifteen agonizing minutes later, Rachel and Hazel emerged in the lobby. Benedict, holding the letter, moved towards them, but then a sudden grip on his elbow from behind brought him to an abrupt halt in his tracks. Startled, he turned and found himself face to face with Victor. Victor looked somber and menacing at the same time. He firmly seized Benedict, twisting his hands behind his back, while Udai came forward and skillfully withdrew the letter clenched between Benedict's fingers.

Udai quickly went through the letter. After absorbing the contents, he requested Victor to release Benedict from the immobilizing grip. He passed on the letter to Victor for him to go through. Rachel and Hazel huddled around Victor to read the letter and furrows formed on their brows as they went through its content.. The atmosphere was tense as they sensed the gravity of the situation.

Victor turned towards Benedict and gently placed his hands on his shoulder. In a calm yet determined voice, he instructed Benedict to lead him to William. For it was only William who held the key to unmasking the true identity of the elusive boss, therefore he must be nabbed immediately without wasting time.

While the men, led by Benedict, left the hotel, Rachel and Hazel retreated into their room. Aware of the dangers and urgency of the matters, they felt unnerved and even contemplated asking for help from Mihir and his powerful dad, the members of Illuminav. However, this move would imply revealing the true identity of Victor and also their relationship with him, which was not desirable so they dismissed the plan, leaving everything at the hands of Victor and fate.

CHAPTER TWENTY-NINE
FALLING IN LOVE WITH THE ENEMY

A palpable tension hung in the air as Victor, Udai and Benedict, entered William's room. William lay in deep slumber, unaware of the reality that awaited him. The men gathered at his bedside, contemplating the next moves. The room echoed with silence before the storm as the men prepared for ensuing confrontation. Without wasting any time, Victor started searching the room, looking for secrets and clues, and instructed Benedict and Udai to search the contents of Walter's laptop, checking the files and folders.

William, in the mean time began squirming and twitching, showing signs of waking up. The three men watched as William struggled to sit up and tried opening his heavy eyelids, his face contorted with the hangover of the night before. Victor decided to assist him, and lifting him to a sitting position on the bed, he put a glass of water to his mouth. William took a few mouthfuls and slowly opened his eyes to find himself face to face with the three men in the room.

Panicking, William instinctively reached for his pistol, but to his dismay, it had gone missing. He looked furtively around the room and saw Benedict, bent over the laptop, appearing peaceful as he worked on it. Clearly, Benedict had changed sides and was now working for the enemies...or had he changed sides much before without arousing his suspicion? The question boggled William. William was now a lone figure and any attempt to resist or fight back single handedly would only be futile. Realizing he was outnumbered and cornered, William resigned himself to the situation, settling for mercy or judgment of these men.

Victor, placing his hand on William's shoulder and tightening the grip, spoke with stern yet calm authority, "Easy there, William. No sudden moves. Tell us what is the plan? We need answers and we need them now."

William looked at Victor with blank eyes and remained tight lipped. William's silence spurred Victor to put forth more questions, "William, talk. What's your boss, Walter's next move? Where is he?"

William hesitated, his mind fuzzy caught in this unexpected turn of events in the web of deception. The lack of clarity due to failed attempts to reach out to the boss, only added to his agony. William was in a highly vulnerable situation. Victor's volley of questions, the intimidating five W's..., Who, When, What, Where and Which seemed like daggers drawn at him. The silence in the room further pressed on him, urging him to reveal the secrets he had guarded so closely.

Benedict, concerned and impatient, looked at William and spoke up,

"Walter, tell them everything they ask. May be we can find a way out of this mess together."

Victor, keeping a watchful eye on William, added,

"You can end this, William. It's time to come clean. No more games, no more deceptions. Time is running out William. The choices you make now will determine your fate."

The air in the room crackled with tension as they awaited William's decision, aware that unfolding events would have far-reaching consequences for all involved. William glanced around the room, realizing there was no way he could escape. He understood the gravity of the situation and with a resigned sigh, he began to spill the beans.

William began unraveling the complex web of deceit spun by Walter. He also revealed the reasons behind the deep-rooted vendetta that had been fueling Walter's actions against Victor. In a somber voice William disclosed,

"Nine years ago, Walter and Victor, comrades on a joint IA assignment in the terrorist infested valley, got cornered by armed assailants and a gunshot severely injured Walter, rendering him incapacitated, unable to move. In the midst of the shooting and chaos, Victor abandoned Walter in injured condition and fled from the scene. He ran away and escaped, leaving his wounded colleague behind."

The three men in the room breathed deeply and steeled themselves to listen to the rest of the story William was about to disclose. William continued with the narration in grave tone,

"The aftermath for Walter was harrowing. He was captured by the terrorists and subjected to severe torture for months in their camp. Waltor contracted various diseases during this period of captivity which left him weak and depressed. Walter holds Victor solely responsible for his suffering, firmly believing that Victor had betrayed him when he needed his help the most. Victor had a choice...to save Walter or complete the mission. He chose the mission, sacrificing Walter for the mission's success. To this day Walter has not forgiven Victor for abandoning him and is living to avenge the betrayal. Walter firmly believes that Victor does not deserve the reputation and position he presently enjoys in the IA."

Victor's facial muscle tightened as he listened intently to Walter's disclosure and he felt restless as the troubling memories of the past resurfaced.

Udai leaned back, processing the information. It was an undisputed fact that betrayal within their own ranks cut deeper than any external threat.

Absorbing the gravity of the revelation, Udai asked in a demanding voice.

"So, Walter's vendetta is fueled by personal grievances against Victor. But there's more to the story, isn't there?"

William, full of remorse, replied, choosing his words carefully,

The Raging Vortex

"In Walter's eyes, Victor's proposed promotion is not justified. It's a position for which Walter is most qualified for and suited. Therefore, this injustice needed correction."

William went on with his narration in the same tone,

"Walter kept looking for an opportunity to take revenge on Victor and the opportunity presented itself in the form of Benedict. When Walter discovered Benedict, Victor's unsuspecting look-alike, a vengeful plot formed in Walter's scheming mind. Walter manipulated Benedict, posing as a filmmaker interested in launching him into the film industry, while in reality he only intended to use him as a pawn in his secret scheme."

William shocked everyone with his string of revelations, and he didn't stop there but kept disclosing in the same monotone,

"To further intensify his scheme, Walter used voice synthesizers and digital advancements to deceive everyone into believing that an underworld don had gained control over the film production, direction, casting, distribution rights etc, etc. This fabrication was a means to manipulate his associates, making them believe they were working under the directives of a powerful underworld figure, and Walter had no say and wasn't responsible for the changes in script, plot, location, set, etc."

Finally, William made the biggest disclosure,

"The latest and the most damaging element of Walter's vengeful plan involves the creation of a video filled with lies and fabrications. Walter plans to release this video on the internet and make it public. He believes it will be a final blow, the end of Victor's credibility and career."

Beads of sweat formed on Walter's forehead as he made the final revelation. Victor looked at him with a fixed gaze while shifting his posture to dissipate the stress built up during the last few minutes.

Udai, always vigilant and astute, probed further,

"Where is Walter? We need to stop him before he unleashes this video."

William, earnest to the core, laid bare the secrets,

"Walter is in a secure location in Delhi. Only he knows where it is. But I can contact him now over a call and you can trace it. I can also discuss his plan further on with him, over the call. But, in return you must pardon me and spare my dignity. Just like Benedict, I've been also deceived by Walter, and coerced into this double game."

Victor, after listening to William's revelations, felt heavy with remorse, realizing the adversities Walter had to face, although he was not in any way responsible for it. Victor decided, it was high time to clear the misunderstandings and loosen the deep-rooted grudges that Walter had been holding on to over the years. Victor instructed William to make a call to Walter. He hoped to talk to him, instill good sense, mend the strained ties, and perhaps seek redemption too.

William positioned himself in front of the laptop, swiftly typing in the required password, initiating the connection. The call connected, but went unanswered, leaving an air of suspense and concern. William tried again, but ended up with the same result. William in frustration, muttered to himself,

"Come on, Walter. Answer the damn call. It's approaching midnight in Delhi; almost the time we are usually supposed to talk and discuss the course of action."

Victor, seated nearby, couldn't shake off the heaviness in his heart. The revelation about Walter's suffering and misunderstood motives weighed on him.

As William continued, trying to connect to Walter, Victor's thoughts wandered back to that fateful night in the valley. Gripped by melancholy he began sharing his side of the story aloud,

"That night, Walter and I had taken shelter in one of the trenches as terrorists were out checking every house to nab us. There had been an intelligence leak, revealing our real identity and hide-out. We could hear the gunshots and commotion coming from the village nearby and we kept hiding in the trench for most part of the night. During the wee hours of the morning, the sounds ceased and just as we got out of the trench, there was another fresh round of gunshots and I saw Walter was hit in the leg. He tried to move but fell back into the trench. At the same time, I realized that one of the terrorist catching sight of me was approaching in our

direction, so I started running away from the trench to lure the terrorist after me. That was the only way to keep injured Walter undetected by the terrorist. I had intended to later return and help Walter. But when I came back after deceiving the terrorist, Walter was not there in the trench. He was gone."

Victor's face bore the burden of regret, and the room resonated with the echoes of a past shrouded in mystery.

Victor continued, reflecting on that night's incident nine years back,

"I reported him missing to our seniors and soon I got caught up in new assignments that took all of my time and attention. Thereafter, series of ongoing missions, back-to-back, kept me busy and I lost track. I never knew what happened to him after that night. It seems he's been nursing grudges over the years, thinking I abandoned him"

The weight of past decisions and misunderstandings bore down on Victor.

Udai nodded, and added...

"Obviously, Walter doesn't know the whole story. He needs to hear the truth."

Victor, grappling with his own guilt nodded in agreement. He realized the urgency to reach out to Walter.

William was serious as he listened to Victor's side of the story and he now pondered over the part destiny had played, prodding Walter and Victor down divergent paths. The masquerading act of fate and the complexity of the emotions entwined in the mission was overwhelming. All the remorse that William had been harboring against Victor was dissipating, the fog of misunderstanding and judgment clearing up. To this day he had shared with Walter the notion that Victor was a cold-heart who had left his colleague, Walter in lurch, and literally walked over his dead body. Victor in their opinion was a cold calculating schemer, driven solely by vaulting ambition, believing in beating all competition to rise up in ranks, and be the sole claimant of the top coveted positions. However, now that the truth was out, William realized that the grave misconception that Walter had been holding needed to be clarified. Undoubtedly, redemption though a distance away, certainly was a necessary goal. "But, why the hell, Walter was not answering the call," William muttered to himself.

As Walter remained unresponsive, Victor's intuition guided him to Vyom.

"Vyom might, with his incredible psychic powers, offer some insight, and even help in mediating a conversation with Walter," Victor shared his view to Udai in somber tone.

Victor took out his phone to make a call to Vyom, but the sudden and abrupt cry of William startled him, causing him to pause mid-dial. William, appearing shocked, sprung up from the chair, pointed towards the screen of the laptop, and exclaimed aloud,

"Oh no, it's Walter. He is in serious condition ..., his house is on fire. Look at this headline flashing on the screen... a house in Hauz Khas, Delhi engulfed in flames. That man whom firefighters are taking out from the ill-fated house looks exactly like Walter! It's Walter for sure, he needs help!"

Victor, Benedict, and Udai looked at the screen with their mouths agape. As they absorbed the distressing reality of the news, beads of sweat appeared on their temples. Burrows etched on their forehead, mirroring the intensity of their concern. Indeed, the man being rescued from the house was Walter, weakened and pallid, he laid unconscious in the arms of firefighters. A strange kind of hush befell in the room as the four men grappled with the shock of the news.

Time seemed to stand still and in that suspended moment, unspoken prayer permeated the room, Victor silently prayed for Walter's safety a return to consciousness. The world outside faded and he hoped for a positive outcome, clinging to the belief that Walter would emerge from this perilous situation unscathed.

Victor, by now too worked up trying to control his emotions, finally began praying aloud, overcome by the weight of worry for Walter,

"Dear God, I implore you to watch over Walter, keep him safe and grant him the strength to overcome this situation," Victor's voice resonated in the room.

Benedict, standing nearby, observed this unexpected display of empathy with skepticism and couldn't contain his surprise. Breaking the silence, he questioned,

"Victor, why are you praying for Walter? He's the one who tried to ruin you, even tried to take your life. Why extend kindness to enemy? He is evil, full of vengeance. He is getting the punishment he deserves."

Victor turned to face Benedict, his expression calm yet resolute and he spoke in a deep voice full with emotions.

"Benedict, people aren't purely good or purely evil. They usually fall in a spectrum. Walter may have done wrong, but that does not mean he is inherently evil and deserves only punishment. We all have our demons and, we all including Walter are silently fighting daily battles within ourselves. In certain situations, circumstances may push us to the edge, allowing the darkness within to momentarily take control. But that doesn't mean we are inherently evil, devoid of goodness and virtue."

Victor continued, his eyes holding a mix of compassion and conviction.

"Walter is a man of worth. We can't overlook his virtues and past services. He's been a victim of misfortune, a pawn of destiny, unwillingly pushed on a treacherous journey that lead him to his own doom. If we were in his shoes, we can't say for sure that we wouldn't have made similar mistakes.

Life is not that simple, and invariably, most of the actions can't be compartmentalised as just black and white with certainty. It has its greys. Basically life is all about understanding and embracing its complexities in its various hues and colours...black, white, grey, VIBGYOR, and any shade in between. Life is about being inclusive. We must not forget the virtues and goodness that exist in everyone. Remember, all holy books teach us to love our enemies and treat them with respect. It's only in understanding and forgiveness that we find the true essence of compassion and humanity."

Benedict, absorbing Victor's perspective, remained silent for a moment before finally saying,

"It's a difficult concept to grasp, Victor. But I guess you're right. Life is more than just black and white."

Victor nodded,

"Indeed, Benedict. It's a kaleidoscope of colors, and in each shade, there's a story waiting to be understood and acknowledged."

Having said so, Victor, with a sense of urgency, quickly dialed Vyom's number. The call connected, and after a few rings, Vyom's composed voice greeted him,

"Hey, Victor, what's up ?"

Victor began, urgency lacing his words,

"Vyom, I need your help right now. Can you spare some time?"

Vyom, sensing the desperation, responded,

"You can always count on me, Victor. I'm here for you. Why don't you drive to my place and we'll discuss the issue in the privacy of home."

Victor, without hesitation, agreed and headed alone towards Vyom's residence, instructing Udai to stay behind and book the earliest flight tickets for seven to New Delhi. They must head for Delhi urgently. The scene of mishappening required proper scrutiny, and above all, Walter required personal care and special security.

CHAPTER THIRTY
THE JUGGERNAUT FEAT

Victor reached Vyom's residence, anxiety etched on his face. He found Vyom in his meditation room, surrounded by the soft glow of crystal lamps. A fine cadence of serene chants resonated from him. There was a sublime aura around him and a magnetic attraction that inspired awe. He was truly a juggernaut of a kind with immense psychic powers and healing touch.

"Vyom, I need your help," Victor exclaimed, interrupting Vyom's meditation.

Vyom opened his eyes, looking at Victor with a calm demeanor.

"What happened, Victor? You seem distressed."

Taking a deep breath, Victor began recounting the entire episode involving himself and Walter. The gravity of the situation reflected in Vyom's expressions as he listened intently.

"I need your help, Vyom. My colleague, Walter is in critical condition. The fire in his house has left him unconscious struggling for life, and the doctors are uncertain about his recovery. I believe your spiritual healing powers can make a difference."

Vyom listened attentively, his demeanor a blend of empathy and determination. He nodded,

"I'll do whatever I can to help," he asserted, his gaze unwavering.

Victor's relief was palpable as Vyom agreed to assist. "Thank you, Vyom. Your help means everything."

Victor explained the urgency of the situation.

"We need to get to Delhi immediately, Vyom. The sooner we can attend to Walter, the better. We must closely examine the scene of mishap, and attend to Walter personally."

Vyom agreed without hesitation,

"I'm with you Victor. We'll do everything in our power to help Walter heal."

The urgency in Victor's eyes was met with a resolute determination in Vyom's.

Victor's phone buzzed with a message...,Udai had succeeded in booking the tickets for the flight and it was to take off in four hours from now. But only five tickets could be booked so that meant Rachel and Hazel had to stay behind in NYC till further booking.

Victor spoke excitedly,

"We're boarding the flight to Delhi that's taking off in four hours. We need to make arrangements and pack up for leaving in just half an hour."

The duo rushed to the airport where they were joined by Udai, William, and Benedict. In the midst of boarding passes and security checks, they discussed their strategy.

As the plane soared over the clouds, Victor watched the city lights of New York gradually diminish and fade in the horizon. Beside him, Vyom remained deep in thought, a sense of purpose etched on his serene face. He had closed his eyes, perhaps centering himself, readying to deploy his spiritual prowess. He was known to be capable of providing distance Reiki to the ailing, allowing healing energy to transcend both time and distance, clearing blockages, from a far.

Meanwhile in Delhi, The Intensive Care Unit (ICU) of Safdarjung Hospital hummed with vibrations and sounds of life saving machines as medical professionals worked diligently to stabilize Walter's condition. The urgency in the room was palpable. Walter had been brought in unconscious state, a casualty of acute respiratory syndrome due to prolonged smoke inhalation.

The medical team surrounded Walter, his limp body a testament to his distressed state. The team hooked Walter up to a ventilator. Intravenous lines were established, delivering a combination of fluids and medications to support his blood pressure.

Blood tests had revealed alarming levels of toxic substances coursing through Walter's veins.

One of the doctors explained the situation to his colleagues,

"We are dealing with not only toxins due to smoke but also a significant overdose of opioids - sleeping pills and painkillers. We need to act swiftly to neutralize the effects and support his recovery."

Intravenous lines were revamped to include the delivery of a carefully calibrated mixture of fluids and medications, to counteract the toxic effects, while providing the necessary support for his vital functions. The doctors focused on cleaning Walter's stomach as an immediate measure to mitigate the impact of the toxin overdose. The procedure aimed to remove any remaining remnants of the ingested substances, preventing further absorption into the bloodstream.

Continuous electrocardiogram (ECG) monitoring tracked the electrical activity of Walter's heart. Medications, carefully chosen to stabilize his heart rhythm and enhance cardiac function, were administered through the intravenous lines. Luckily, Walter had escaped any kind of burn injury and had majorly suffered from asphyxiation, due to smoke inhalation besides drug overdose.

Each member of the medical team was making their best effort to stabilize Walter's condition and restore him to conscious state. Vyom too had initiated a remote healing session for Walter, mid-air. Each Juggernaut in their respective field of healing were unleashing their full potentials to revive Walter.

CHAPTER THIRTY ONE
CLINGING ON TO LAST STRAW OF HOPE

With Richard having left for Delhi, back in NYC Hazel and Rachel found themselves anxious and pensive in their hotel room of Westwin. They grappled with the reality that they couldn't accompany Richard. However, they understood the gravity of the situation and circumstances.

"I just hope that everything goes well for them in Delhi,"

Hazel muttered, her mind preoccupied with thoughts of Richard.

"But we can't just sit here,"

Rachel sighed, her voice filled with regret, her brow furrowed with concern. Hazel nodded in agreement.

However, despite the lingering worry they decide to make the most of the remaining four days in the city as per the original itinerary set by Mihir and Udai. They plan to immerse themselves in the ongoing conference, attending sessions, and networking with fellow professionals before leaving for Delhi. As they contemplate their schedule for the following day, Mihir comes in and puts forth an invitation with a warm smile.

"Hazel ma'am, and Rachel, I've been thinking," **Mihir began,**

"why don't you both come and stay at my place for the next four in NYC? My parents would love to have you over, and we can make the most of these days together."

Rachel and Hazel exchanged surprised glances before Hazel replied,

"That's a generous offer, Mihir. But we don't want to impose."

Mihir chuckled, *"It's not an imposition at all. In fact, my parents are eager to host such distinguished guests. They are waiting in the car just outside Westwin. Please, do come."*

Hazel looked at Rachel, and after a brief moment of consideration, Hazel smiled and said

"Alright Mihir. We'd be happy to join you. Tell your parents we appreciate the invitation."

Mihir grinned, relieved and excited.

'*Fantastic! Let's head out."*

With a sense of anticipation, Rachel and Hazel accompanied Mihir to the waiting Rolls Royce. The prospect of spending the remaining days in a more welcoming environment lifted their spirits but they needed to be cautious and mindful about not revealing the fact that Victor was a spy and also about their relationship with him.

As they settled into the plush seats of the luxury car, Athira greeted them warmly,

"Welcome, Rachel and Hazel. We're delighted to have you join us. Make yourselves comfortable."

"Thank you so much for having us," Rachel replied, her anticipation evident in her voice. Hazel nodded in agreement.

As the car rolled on, Marc shared the news, *"I have a business trip to Illinois, Chicago tonight. Athira will be your gracious host in my absence."*

Little did Rachel and Hazel realize, this invitation extended much beyond a simple act of hospitality. Athira was more that eager to know Rachel even better, and moreover she certainly intended to introduce Rachel to the Marc household...their way of living, their customs and beliefs...perhaps also groom her a little in the areas required. After all she was to become her daughter-in-law. Vyom had confirmed Rachel's suitability as Mihir's life partner after studying her aura and vibes during the sundowner earlier in the weekend at Marc's residence. The Marcs greatly regarded Vyom, and valued his words. They always followed his advice.

A doting mother that Athira was, she wanted to see her son happily married to his lady love and settle down early in life. She was looking forward very soon to a grand wedding ceremony of her son with Rachel.

As the journey in the car continued, Athira engaged in casual conversation, subtly gauging Rachel's interests and persona. Meanwhile, Hazel was drawn into conversation with Marc, who shared insights about their family traditions.

The subtle grooming had begun, Athira seamlessly lacing friendly conversations with nuances aimed at acquainting Rachel with the values and culture of the coveted family she would soon be a part of. Rachel and Hazel were delighted with the attention they were getting, and felt at home because of warm and welcoming gestures of Athira and Marc.

It seemed, the dark days were finally getting over and good times were knocking at the door. As such, It's always good to keep clinging on to hope. Even the weakest straw of hope can make the journey called life a little lighter and worth it. Back in Delhi too, doctors sighed with relief as Walter regained consciousness. The ominous specter of danger that loomed over him had dissipated. His condition was stable and doctors declared him out of danger, shifting him to a room in the private ward.

The news of Walter's improved condition sparked a glimmer of hope among those who had been anxiously waiting to meet him. But even after a day of shifting, visitors were prohibited from entering Walter's room. However, this was not a deterrent for William and he found a way to enter the room by trading places with one of the attending male nurses. With practiced demeanor, William entered Walter's room, slipping into the role of male nurse effortlessly. He moved stealthily, avoiding the scrutinizing eyes of the doctors who periodically checked on Walter.

The Raging Vortex

In the hushed atmosphere of the private ward room, Walter lay in hospital bed seeming restful, recovering and regaining strength. As the attending doctors left the room with smiles of satisfaction written on their faces, pleased with Walter's swift recovery, William seized upon the opportunity to orchestrate the secret plan of Victor.

William, after making sure that he was alone in the room with Walter, took cautious glances around and approached Walter. He leaned over and placed his face close to Walter, revealing his true identity, his voice barely above a whisper, "Walter, it's me William. We need to talk. Your plan has worked. You've succeeded."

Walter, momentarily startled, looked up to study the face deeply and quickly realized it was William, his accomplice. He sighed in relief, his voice sounding cheerful,

"So good to see you William."

William wasted no time and started delivering the carefully scripted news.

"Victor has met with an accident," William revealed with a tone of feigned regret. *"He is comatose, and there's little hope for his survival. His wife and daughter haven't bothered to check on him, given his intense hatred for him. Walter, your mission has been successful. Your desire for Victor's doom has been fulfilled,"* William declared with a mix of accomplishment and urgency.

Walter's steady gaze remained focused on William as he grasped and analyzed the gravity of the news conveyed by William. For a full twenty seconds he didn't respond, his face remained devoid of any emotion and then he finally muttered,

"What have I done?"

A tinge of regret was palpable in his voice.

Surprisingly, instead of joy and satisfaction, Walter's face bore the look of guilt and self loathing. The taste of victory was bitter, and the weight of guilt settled upon him like an unshakable burden.

The weight of his vengeful plot pressed down on him, and remorse flooded his conscience.

"I've achieved what I wanted, but it feels wrong. I've crossed a line, William. God will never forgive me for what I've done,"

Walter confessed, his voice heavy with remorse."

"Is there anything I can do for Victor?"

Walter asked.

"I want to make amends. Can we contact Hazel and Rachel, reveal my vengeful plot, and seek their forgiveness? I want them to be at Victor's side during these times when he needs them the most."

William, understanding the depth of Walter's regret, listened attentively and nodded agreeing to act upon his wishes,

"I'll do as you wish, Walter."

He then added,

"I know of a powerful spiritual healer who has done miracles. We can employ his services to aid in Victor's recovery. His name is Vyom. I'll talk to him and discuss how to proceed in this direction."

Walter, visibly broken and repentant, sought assurance from William.

"Can Vyom really bring Victor out of a coma?"

William in a reassuring tone replied,

"Vyom has a remarkable reputation for reviving people back from has a proven track record. He will surely help Victor out of coma." He gave him a cheerful smile, *"Rest easy Walter. We're on the right path."*

William, then helped Walter in lying down supine and administered the needful placebos and prescription drugs, ensuring that Walter was at peace and comfortably rested.

With that William left the room, hoping Walter gets the needful restorative deep-sleep. He was feeling satisfied that Victor's plan, with the goal of achieving reconciliation had been successfully executed. This plan was their last straw of hope and they were counting on it and were clinging to it. Much to everybody's expectations, Walter, lying in the quiet confines of his room, was praying for Victor's recovery and hoping for a better future for both of them. The journey towards redemption and forgiveness had begun. Hope, not lost, was bearing fruits.

CHAPTER THIRTY-TWO
THE PHOENIX ARISEN

As the sun heralded a new day, Victor readied himself to initiate the next phase of his intricate plan that required William and Vyom to take the lead. It unfolded with William entering into Walter's room along with Vyom and introducing the enigmatic spiritual healer to a curious Walter. Walter, awestruck by the intense aura emanating from Vyom, looked at him wide-eyed. There was a certain serenity in Vyom's demeanor that seemed to transcend the confines of time and space. Walter was momentarily spellbound by the enigmatic Vyom.

With practiced ease, Vyom initiated a conversation, effortlessly drawing Walter into a dialogue that flowed like a gentle stream meandering through the landscape of his thoughts. Words became bridges connecting their worlds, walls were broken and bonds were forged. Walter poured out his heart, recounting the scars of his past and the depths of his present turmoil.

Walter, overwhelmed by Vyom's charisma, found himself compelled to confide in the spiritual healer, baring his innermost fears and recent misdoing…the malevolent designs driven by revenge and jealousy. He expressed his yearning for redemption and articulated his sincere desire to see Victor resurrected from coma.

Vyom, greatly moved by Walter's vulnerabilities, embarked on the mission to restore Walter to his original good health and cheer. For this Walter must first clear up the haze of doubt and misunderstanding that had been clouding Walter's peace of mind over the years.

Vyom invited Walter to embark on a journey of memories through the eyes of the mind and revisit the tumultuous night in the valley, unraveling the whole picture with moments of truth and revelation. As Walter drifted into the hypnotic sleep under the guidance of Vyom, the night of the tempest unfolded in his mind revealing the whole incident like scenes from a movie with every twist and turn. Walter could see the terrorists coming towards the trench where he lay injured, unable to move and how daring Victor led the terrorists into a chase after himself that spared incapacitated Walter from being detected and shot to death by the terrorists on the spot, that very moment itself. Walter witnessed the events of the fateful night with newfound clarity, each detail etched in the canvas of his mind. And as the journey drew to a close, Walter emerged from the depths of the hypnotic sleep with Vyom's guidance.

The truth had emerged from the shadows, casting a harsh light on Walter's misconceptions and misplaced vengeance. With a dawning realization, Walter came face to face with the consequences of his actions - the toll they had taken on Victor, who lay in coma, teetering on the brink of life and death. In that moment of clarity, he recognized the magnitude of his mistake - how his thirst for revenge had nearly cost Victor his life. A wave of surmounting remorse washed over Walter, With a heavy heart, Walter vowed to right his wrongs, to atone for the pain he had inflicted.

Turning to Vyom with a plea born of desperation and remorse, Walter beseeched him to use his psychic powers to heal Victor, to restore him to health and wholeness. For this he offered Vyom a share of his considerable wealth as a token of gratitude.

With a solemn nod, Vyom accepted Walter's request to initiate a healing session for Victor. Vyom promised Walter that Victor, their hero, would surely rise, phoenix-like, towards the end of the day. He even went on to assure that by tomorrow evening both Walter and Victor would be fit and strong enough to go for a walk together, out in the boulevards of South Delhi, all by themselves. Phoenix arisen..., seemed to be the forecast made by Vyom.

Walter, with renewed hope watched, as Vyom sat down on the floor cross-legged, eyes shut. He shifted almost instantaneously into a state of deep meditation, in what seemed like a trance. Soon, the whole room pulsated with an energy that transcended the ordinary. Vyom, determined to demonstrate his prowess, initiated a healing session for Walter first. He channelised his psychic powers to uplift Walter's sinking spirit and enhance his physical strength. Walter, after witnessing the transformative effects on himself, was filled with reverence and gratitude. Walter, now patiently watched as Vyom started the distant healing session for Victor.

Even as Vyom made a convincing show of initiating the act of distant healing sessions for Victor, doubts did gnaw at his heart. He hoped to convince a seasoned player like Walter with this deceptive act of his.

Meanwhile, at that moment, Victor, in his secret enclave, was busy with sessions of meetings with the investigating team that had studied the scene of fire. It was confirmed that a short circuit had indeed led to the inferno. The timely action of fire-fighters had controlled the fire from spreading over to the floor where Walter resided.

Although Walter was found in an unconscious state, engulfed in a heavy blanket of smoke (that had bellowed up from the floor below) the hospital's medical test report however, pointed out towards the fact that Walter must have already passed out due to drug overdose , even before respiratory distress syndrome due to smoke inhalation subsequently took over. Medical reports showed high levels of toxins in Walter's blood that usually result from an overdose of opioids and NSAIDS. Immediately after the meeting with the investigating team Victor embarked upon a special training session with Benedict. The training aimed at molding Benedict into a spy. Victor truly believed that Benedict possessed the basic traits of a spy, and with a little bit of honing of the skills he would make for a perfect spy. Victor, determined upon initiating Benedict into the covert world of espionage, was training him for functioning as an asset, informer or operator.

Benedict was young, talented, intelligent, and disciplined. But it was not merely his intellect that had caught Victor's attention; it was Benedict's fairly strong character, unwavering commitment to his principles, dedication to his ideals of patriotism and nationalism that set him apart. These convictions provided him with an unshakable moral compass, most important for navigating in the murky world of espionage. In Benedict, Victor saw not only a promising recruit, but a potential asset of unparalleled value. Benedict's ideals provided a solid foundation for making of a great spy by further honing of the required skill sets. It was an undeniable fact that Benedict's tumultuous past and life of adversities had turned him remarkably mature beyond his age. He yearned for a meaningful life aligned with a greater purpose...that of serving his country; which Victor was quick to assess and address. Our wise man, Victor therefore devoted his time and attention to connect with Benedict psychologically. After having gained Benedict's admiration and confidence, Victor used his motivational skills to influence Benedict, making him a willing candidate ready to undergo training and then foray into the world of espionage, to serve his country as a spy. Spy, the silent, unseen guardian of the nation's security.

As a spy, Benedict must be ready to brave dangers for the greater good, walk the razor's edge between truth and deception, make sacrifices known only to a few; yet these are the sacrifices that are supreme and keep the nation secure and strong. Benedict must ready himself for the flight of the phoenix. endure hardship and pain, and dare to see death eye to eye.

CHAPTER THIRTY-THREE
THE PERFECT IMPERFECT FRAGILE LIFE

Even as Benedict's training session with Victor was keeping the two men in Delhi more than busy, several thousand miles away in NYC, a serene scene unfolded in Athira's cozy living room. Mihir, Rachel, Athira and Hazel, seated comfortably, were engrossed in a heartfelt conversation. Updates over the phone calls from Udai this morning, had confirmed the well-being of the two men, Victor and Walter; a news that brought a wave of relief to all concerned. Udai also informed that almost all of the pressing issues had been resolved and as such Hazel and Rachel could look forward to a happy family reunion upon landing in Delhi, the day after tomorrow.

Hazel, Rachel, Mihir, and Athira, now relieved of tensions after hearing this much awaited good news engage in a heart-to-heart conversation. They talk about a whole lot of stuff, reminiscing about their innocent childhood and the adventures of their college days. Their laughter filled the living room, painting the scene with an aura of warmth and camaraderie.

Seizing the moment, Hazel extended an invitation to Athira to speak on the occasion of the convocation day ceremony of her college as a guest speaker. Athira graciously accepted the invitation and expressed her desire to forge a deeper long lasting relationship with the reputed institute. She evinced an interest in allocating grants for funding scholarships and research. Athira, as a trustee of 'Atharva Foundation' (Corporate Social Responsibility arm of the Atharva Pharmaceuticals) and founder of the 'Athira Museum of Art and Handicraft' held a great reputation as a philanthropist and an Indian art collector. Her Foundation supported programs in the areas of healthcare, education, women empowerment, and rural development. As such, she could not let go off, this wonderful opportunity of association with a premier educational institute..., making possible, yet another contribution in the field of higher education.

Hazel and Athira, pleased over discovering shared passions and common grounds, felt a connect and shifted their conversation to a more personal level, planning the engagement ceremony of Mihir and Rachel. The prospect of combining the upcoming Christmas festivities, the holiday celebrations with Mihir and Rachel's engagement ceremony filled them with excitement and anticipation.

Mihir, observing the two women lost in lively conversation, couldn't help but feel a sense of joy seeing them bond like old friends. Rachel, too, shared in the happiness, noting how her mother seemed more carefree and relaxed than ever before. Mihir and Rachel were brimming with joy. They had every reason to be happy; after all, their love affair and decision to marry had received the approval of their parents. Feeling fortunate to have received unconditional love and support from their parents in every aspect of their lives... be it their careers, pursuits of passions, or now, in sanctioning their love and planning their grand wedding... they couldn't ask for more.

Rachel's thoughts soon meandered towards the impending journey. She beckoned her mom to start packing for boarding the flight to Delhi. The prospect of returning to their home filled her with excitement. For years she had yearned for the day when her small loving family would be together again under one roof, a dream that had sustained her through countless lonely nights. She had greatly missed her father, and carried his memory like a precious treasure, like a beacon of hope guiding her through the darkest of times. And now, finally, after what felt like an eternity of waiting, her dream of seeing her family united in their home was about to become a reality.

Meanwhile, Hazel's face radiated with happiness as she packed her belongings. With a lightness in her step and song in her heart, she prepared for the journey back to Delhi, where she would at last find solace in the loving arms of Richard. After years of yearning, their small sweet family would be whole once more, united in the warmth of their home. The thought of finally being one with Richard, whom she had missed dearly, filled her with an indescribable joy. She couldn't help but reflect upon her life journey thus far, and reached a conclusion..., we humans are but pawns of destiny. We like to think that we can take charge of the future by planning for it, and that, if we keep making concerted effort in the right direction with a set goal, we can be masters of our fate. But the fact is that life has its own way of taking over and changing our path towards the destined, no matter how best we plan and try. With time we however realize, God's plan is the best plan.

Back in Delhi, Victor eagerly awaited the arrival of Hazel and Rachel. Even amidst the whirlwind of the ongoing training sessions with Benedict and intense schedule, Victor's heart danced with joy in anticipation of a long-awaited reunion with his beloved family. Victor had too many reasons to be happy. His renewed camaraderie with Walter, indeed, added to the layer of fulfillment to his happiness. Moreover, as if by fate's design, Victor's name was finally announced for the prestigious post of Directorship of 'The Intelligence Academy'. This promotion came to Victor as a pleasant surprise, adding greatly to his sense of contentment and accomplishment.

As Victor prepared to embark on this new chapter of his career, he couldn't help but feel a profound sense of gratitude for the blessing that had come his way. He pondered upon the journey of his life thus far. The journey had indeed been marred by many rough patches. And, no doubt, life had been tough on him..., had pushed him over the edge too many times, thrown him into the raging vortex but he had survived living this perfectly imperfect fragile life. However, now at this moment today, if at all... all of it seemed surreal and sweet... worthwhile and satisfying! He had all the reasons to thank God!! Tomorrow was filled with promises for a beautiful day when he would have the love of his life, Rachel and

Hazel in his loving embrace, within the warm folds of their cozy home.... something he had been yearning for over twenty long years. He was really proud of Hazel and Rachel... they had beaten all odds to emerge as stalwarts in their respective fields by sheer dint of their talent and dedication. They were truly awesome human beings, beautiful and bold, having courage and conviction, defying the limitations and constraints of circumstances, growing in face of challenges to emerge stronger and loving. Indeed, they were inspiring and exemplary...truly Anahatas, the unbeaten pawns of destiny...Richard, Hazel, Rachel, Udai, Walter, Benedict... all.

www.ingramcontent.com/pod-product-compliance
Ingram Content Group UK Ltd.
Pitfield, Milton Keynes, MK11 3LW, UK
UKHW020244240426
12048UKWH00026B/1594